THE BITTER WITH
THE SWEET

A SWEET COVE MYSTERY BOOK 15

J. A. WHITING

To hear about new books and book sales, please sign up for my mailing list at:

www.jawhitingbooks.com

❀ Created with Vellum

For my family with love

1

———

Angie Roseland carried four boxes of baked goods while Mr. Finch held open the door to the Pirate's Den restaurant on the main street of the little seaside town of Sweet Cove. Finch balanced his cane in one hand and a bag of fudge in the other.

The owner, Bessie Lindquist, hurried over to take two boxes from the load Angie was carrying. "Morning. Thank heavens you could bring extra desserts. We've been flat out busy. Busier than ever for this time of year. I don't know what secret ingredients you put in these sweets, but the customers clamor for them." Bessie was a short, petite woman who had owned the restaurant with her husband for over twenty years.

"Morning, Angie ... Mr. Finch." Bessie's husband, Art, came out from the kitchen to help with the boxes. "You're looking fine," he told Angie. "Married life must agree with you."

When Angie chuckled, her blue eyes sparkled. "I'm a lucky woman."

"And that Josh Williams is a very lucky man. His waistband is going to increase in size with a talented baker for a wife and two candy store owners in the family." Art took the bag from Finch. "This fudge from your candy store is a big hit. We've been putting a piece on the plate whenever we serve the fresh fruit for dessert."

"How's Josh doing?" Bessie asked.

"He's healing well. Almost back to normal," Angie told them. Josh had been injured while rescuing an older man and woman from a burning house and he'd nearly lost his life by racing into the inferno to save them.

"Just a bit of a limp remaining in one of his legs." Mr. Finch smiled and lifted his cane. "Josh is in good company."

"That he is," Bessie agreed. "Do you two have time for some coffee?"

"Afraid not." Angie handed off the remaining

boxes to the restaurant owner. "We've got a few more deliveries to make and then I need to get back to the bake shop."

"I heard the museum has asked you to consider creating a satellite bake shop on the premises," Bessie said. "It sounds like a great opportunity to expand."

"It is." Angie placed the receipt for the baked goods on the counter so Bessie could sign it. "I'm just not sure if now is the right time."

"Give it some thought," Bessie said. "It might not be something you want to pass up. Heck, we wish the museum invited us to put a small Pirate's Den inside the place."

After a little more chat, Finch and Angie left the restaurant and got back into the van to finish making the deliveries.

"News travels fast," Angie said.

"Indeed, it does. The whole town must know by now about the museum's offer to you." Finch leaned on his cane as he stepped into the passenger seat.

"What do you think of the offer?" Angie asked the man. "I don't want to spread myself too thin and it wasn't long ago I promoted Louisa to assistant manager of the bake shop."

"Louisa is a smart woman and an excellent worker," Finch said. "She can handle the new responsibilities with ease which will give you time to open the new place without worries."

Angie nodded as she pulled the van away from the curb. "It's true. I don't know why I'm not jumping at this. I want to expand, but something is making me hesitate."

Finch glanced at the young woman. "Do you sense something?"

Letting out a long sigh, Angie's shoulders drooped. "I wish I didn't, but I do. I haven't brought it up because I hoped it would go away." Taking a quick look at Finch, she asked, "Do you feel it?"

Mr. Finch adjusted his black framed glasses. "It's been floating on the air the past two days. I don't think it's something we'll be able to avoid."

Angie let out a soft groan. "Never a dull moment."

"Don't let whatever is about to happen stop you from expanding the bake shop to a new location, Miss Angie. We are together and we will give you the help you need."

Angie's lips turned up in a smile. "I don't know what I'd do without you, my sisters, and Josh."

"And Tom and Jack and Rufus," Finch added the

names to the list of family and friends. "Not to mention the two fine felines."

Turning the steering wheel to make a turn onto a street running off of Main, Angie shook her head with a smile. "I should have put Euclid and Circe at the very top of the list."

The van stopped at the end of the driveway to *Room and Board*, the Sweet Cove boarding house run for the past fifteen years by Maribeth Perkins, a tall, thin, woman in her mid-sixties with short blond hair. Places like the boarding house, although common in the nineteenth century, were few and far between now. The large house allowed renters to lease a suite of rooms and have access to the common areas ... the kitchen, living room, and sunroom. It was distinct from a bed and breakfast as the residents rented long-term, some for months at a time and others for years.

It was a popular place for medical and graduate students to live as well as a few single women and men and several elderly. A big porch stretched across the front of the house and there were gardens in the backyard along with shade trees and different places to sit. A sweeping veranda on the left side of the house provided spectacular views of the cliffs and ocean beyond. Breakfast was served every morning as part of the rental fee and on Wednesday evenings Maribeth prepared dinner for the residents to enjoy together. The woman had contracted with Angie to provide breakfast breads and muffins and some desserts.

Mr. Finch leaned on his cane while Angie checked the boxes for the ones going to the boarding house. Handing a brown dessert box to Finch, the young woman gathered two more and shut the hatch. Before starting for the house, Angie paused as a rush of adrenaline raced through her body preventing her from advancing.

"Miss Angie?" Finch asked with concern after seeing the expression on her face.

Angie shook herself and forced a smile. "I ... I don't know. I felt funny for a second."

She and Finch started for the walkway to the front of the house when the door flew open and Maribeth hurried onto the porch with a wild look in her eyes.

When she noticed the two people coming up the walk, she yelled to them. "Help me! Please hurry!"

Angie jogged ahead as Finch dashed for the steps, his limp more evident as his pace quickened.

"What's wrong?" Angie asked.

"Inside. One of the boarders." Maribeth's hand

pressed against her chest. "Oh. I need to call emergency. We need an ambulance." The woman's face was ghostly pale and her flustered behavior suggested she might be in a state of shock.

"Tell me what happened." Angie tried to get Maribeth to describe the emergency. "Shall we go in? Who needs help?"

Mr. Finch didn't wait for an explanation, instead opening the door and stepping into the foyer of the big house. "Hello? Can I be of help?"

Maribeth hurried inside with Angie at her heels.

"He can't answer you, Mr. Finch. Perry is unconscious." Maribeth wrung her hands.

"Show us," Angie's voice was firm.

Maribeth stumbled through the house to the back hallway and entered one of the boarder's rooms. Covered with a light blanket, the man lay on his back in his bed near the window wearing a t-shirt. His head rested on his pillow. He looked peaceful as if he was sound asleep and dreaming.

Standing just inside the threshold, Maribeth gestured and whispered. "He won't wake up."

Angie stepped quickly to the bed and touched the young man's neck in an attempt to find a heartbeat. The skin was cold and pearly white. "Did you call 911?"

Maribeth seemed not to understand the question.

"What's going on?" An older man in slacks and a pressed shirt appeared at the door. "What's happened to Perry? Is he ill?"

Finch took out his phone and placed the emergency call while Angie began chest compressions on the man lying in the bed.

A young woman, her hair a mass of long, auburn curls, poked her head into the room. "What's going on? What's happened?" She went to Angie's side and the two took turns doing the compressions.

Before long, the medical personnel arrived, were ushered into the house by a resident, and began to work on the man in the bed as Angie and the auburn-haired woman stepped back. Perspiration glistened on Angie's forehead from anxiety and the exertion of trying to get the man's heart started.

A police officer entered the bedroom and hurriedly asked everyone to assemble in the living room of the house.

"I don't think Perry's going to make it," the auburn-haired woman told Angie with trembling words. As they filed down the hall, she lowered her voice and added, "I think he's already dead."

Angie had the same impression. "Do you live here?"

"My rooms are across from Perry's."

"You knew the young man?"

Tears fell from the woman's eyes. "His name is Perry Wildwood. He's a med student at the university." The woman extended her hand to shake. "I'm Megan Milton."

Mr. Finch stood next to Maribeth trying to comfort the woman. Maribeth swayed a little as she cried and Finch helped her to settle into a comfortable chair. "How did you know the man was ill?" he asked.

Maribeth sniveled into a tissue. "Perry is always up before this. He needs to be at school early. I knocked on his door. When he didn't reply, I opened the door and called his name. I thought he'd overslept."

Angie, Megan, and the older man who had been with them moved closer to Maribeth to hear her tell what had happened.

"Did you try to wake him?" Megan asked.

"Yes." Maribeth's eyes seemed unfocused. "I called his name. When he didn't respond, I went over to the bed to tug on his arm. He felt cold. I...." The woman clutched at her chest. "I got scared. I went out to the porch. I looked for help." Maribeth glanced up at Finch. "Angie and Mr. Finch. They were in the driveway."

"Did you call for an ambulance right away?" the older gentleman asked.

Maribeth blinked. "I forgot to. How foolish. I panicked."

"It happens in situations like this," Angie tried to reassure her. "People's minds go blank. The emergency people are here now."

Finch made eye contact with Angie and they slipped over to the fireplace away from the others.

"Do you find this an odd situation?" Finch whispered his question. "A very young man appears to have died in the night with no sign of a struggle. No drug paraphernalia visible. Alone in his room."

"That doesn't mean he was alone all night," Angie said. "I think we just found out what has been floating on the air picking at us for the past couple of days."

"I think we'll be visiting this boarding house quite often over the coming weeks," Finch said. "I'd better contact Chief Martin."

"No need," Angie told him. "Here he comes."

When Chief Martin entered the foyer and came

into the living room, his eyebrows raised when he spotted Finch and Angie together by the fireplace.

"I'm happy to see you two here. Care to come out to the porch with me and tell me what's been going on?"

"If only we knew," Finch said softly as he and Angie left the house with the chief.

2

————

Standing outside on the wide wraparound porch while the other officers spoke with the owner and residents of the house, Angie and Mr. Finch gave the chief a rundown of what had happened over the last thirty minutes.

Chief Martin rubbed at the side of his face. "So Maribeth didn't call in the emergency right away?"

"She panicked." Mr. Finch held the top of his cane and gently twirled it under his palm.

"Hmm." The chief's lips were turned down. "Maribeth came out to the porch looking for help? Why didn't she call on someone who was in the house? There are people living with her."

Angie's eyebrow raised. "Good question. I guess she really did panic and wasn't thinking straight."

"You were both in the young man's room?" Chief Martin looked at Angie. "You did chest compressions?"

Nodding Angie said, "My impression was that the man was already dead. His skin was very cool to the touch. There were no signs that he was breathing. I think he died hours before Maribeth found him."

"Did either of you feel anything *unusual* when you were in the room?" the chief asked. Chief Martin was well aware that the four Roseland sisters and Mr. Finch had some extrasensory skills and he called on them to help out from time to time with difficult cases. The chief even had an inkling that the two family cats had some special skills, although no one could actually explain those abilities. "I don't understand any of it," the chief would often say, "but I'm more than willing to accept the premise that certain people ... and animals ... are capable of possessing some higher-level *skills* that the common person lacks."

Finch cleared his throat. "I don't believe the young man passed away from natural causes."

"Is this notion a result of logical reasoning?" the chief asked. "Or from *sensing* it?"

"It was something I picked up on when standing in the room," Finch said.

"Angie?" The chief looked to the young woman. "Did you sense anything?"

"Something picked at me. I was rushed trying to revive the man. Maribeth was crying. One of the residents, Megan Milton, came in to help. There were a lot of emotions flying around in there and unfortunately I wasn't able to focus on them to try and sort them out."

"Do I hear a *but* in your voice?" the chief asked.

Angie thought back to the experience of finding Perry Wildwood unconscious. "When I approached the man in his bed and started the chest compressions, I ... got a tiny whiff of something."

"What did it smell like?" Chief Martin took a step closer to Angie who took a few seconds to reply.

"It was sort of like...." Angie's nose scrunched up. "Hair spray? Medicine?"

"Hair spray?" Mr. Finch asked with a puzzled expression.

"You didn't smell it?" Angie asked Finch.

"I did not. I don't believe I noticed any odors on the air."

"Was it on the air in general?" Chief Martin asked. "Or was it coming from the man?"

One side of Angie's mouth turned down. "I'm not sure."

"Okay." The chief nodded appreciatively. "Do the two of you have time to stay for a little while? Maybe mingle with the residents. See what you can find out?"

Angie glanced at Finch. "We can stay for a little while. I'll just text Louisa at the bake shop and let her know I'm running late."

Back inside the house, Angie and Finch joined several residents who had gathered in the large living room where they were talking softly with one another. Megan, a pharmacy student, had reported trying to revive the young man and was fielding questions from the others.

"Did Perry speak?" asked Roger Winthrop, the older man who had come downstairs shortly after Angie and Megan began tending to Perry.

"He was unconscious." Megan didn't want to upset the residents so she didn't mention the fact that she thought Perry was dead when she entered his room.

From the hallway, a police officer closed the pocket doors to the living room so the stretcher carrying Perry Wildwood could be taken out to the waiting ambulance without anyone watching it go.

"Please stay in here for a few minutes," the officer said. "Chief Martin will be in to speak with you soon," the officer said.

"Are we in danger?" Mary Bishop, a seventy-four-year old woman with soft blond hair asked the question with a trembling voice. "Was Perry killed?"

"Killed? Why on earth would you suggest such a thing?" Roger Winthrop asked. "He hasn't been pronounced dead. They may revive him on the way to the hospital. Perry might have some undiagnosed condition that caused him to pass out."

"Like what?" Mary Bishop looked pale.

"Well, anything," Roger said. "Diabetes. A heart issue. Low blood sugar. The flu. There are any number of things that could have caused Perry's collapse."

"How did Perry look when you went in to help him?" Andy Hobbs was a thirty-five-year old, tall, slender nursing student with a short trimmed beard.

"He was on his back," Megan said with tears streaming down her face. "He was very pale."

"Did you check his vitals?" Andy asked.

"No." Megan flustered for a second and then gestured towards Angie. "I saw the other woman do that. We took turns doing compressions."

Andy turned his brown eyes onto Angie. "Did *you* check for a pulse?"

"I tried to," Angie told the small gathering. "But I'm not trained and I was hurrying. I didn't feel a pulse, but that doesn't mean there wasn't one."

"Megan should have checked," Andy scolded the pharmacy student.

"What difference would it have made?" Megan snapped at the man. "We were trying to revive Perry. If he had a faint pulse or not, we would have done the compressions anyway. We didn't know how long he'd been unconscious."

Andy looked at Angie with disdain. "Who are you again?"

Angie bristled at the man's tone and manner. "I'm Angie Roseland. Mr. Finch and I were delivering baked goods when Maribeth called to us for help." Angie straightened and met Andy's piercing look. "Do you know Perry well?"

Andy said, "Me? Not well, no. I've been living in the house for about a year, but our schedules don't match up much. We're always at school or studying."

"You have meals together?" Finch asked.

"Sometimes," Andy explained. "The students in the house usually grab something from the kitchen for breakfast and head out to classes. Once in a while, we're able to make the Wednesday dinners, otherwise we get something at the university or cook something for ourselves when we get back."

"Do any of you know Perry well?" Finch asked.

"Perry was a nice person," Mary Bishop said, but was immediately interrupted by Roger.

"Why use the past tense when you describe Perry?" Roger reprimanded the woman. "We don't know for sure that he has passed on."

Mary glared at the man. "Perry *is* a nice person," she repeated. "He is very nice to talk to. He took the time to get to know us, always asked how we were. He'll make a very kind doctor."

"Is Perry married?" Angie asked.

"No, he isn't," Mary said.

"Does he have a girlfriend?"

"No," Megan said brushing at her eyes with her fingers. "Perry is super busy. He doesn't really have a lot of time to date."

"Where is the young man from?" Finch asked.

"Perry is from Maine," Roger said.

"What about family?"

"He's an only child," Megan said.

"His parents passed away a few years ago," Andy told them.

"Any close relatives?" Angie questioned.

"He has an uncle he's mentioned several times," Mary said.

"How long has Perry lived in the house?" Finch asked.

Megan spoke up. "Perry's a second year med student. He moved in here when he started med school."

"What about the rest of you?" Angie asked. "How long have you lived here?"

"I've been here the longest. Three years for me," Roger said.

"I moved in two years ago," Mary said. "Following the death of my husband."

"I've been living here for almost two years," Megan said.

"Does anyone else live in the house?" Angie asked.

"There's one room open," Roger said. "An elderly resident moved away last month to a nursing home. No one has taken a lease for the room yet."

"Maribeth lives here, of course," Mary pointed out.

Angie nodded. "Does Perry have any enemies?"

Mary's hand flew to her chest. "Enemies?"

"Why do you ask that?" Roger demanded. "Do you think someone tried to hurt Perry?"

"Just wondering about the circumstances of Perry's life," Angie explained.

"Did Perry have any arguments with anyone recently?" Finch asked.

The residents looked at one another and shook their heads or shrugged.

"Perry never said anything about an argument or not getting along with anyone," Megan said. "Perry is well-liked. He gets along with everyone."

Angie thought there was probably someone who didn't get along with Perry since she was pretty sure the young man had died in his room a few hours ago.

The sliding wooden doors opened to reveal a tired-looking Chief Martin who solemnly entered the room with Maribeth Perkins. The woman held the chief's arm and dabbed at her eyes with a tissue.

"For those of you who don't know me, I'm Police Chief Phillip Martin. I'm very sorry to report that your housemate, Perry Wildwood, has passed away."

Gasps went around the room.

Megan sank into a chair and sobbed.

"I knew it." Tears ran down Mary Bishop's face, but her expression was one of anger. "I knew Perry had passed. Was he murdered?"

"What makes you ask that?" the chief questioned.

"He was twenty-five-years old," Mary said brushing at her cheek. "People that age don't just die in their sleep."

"It *is* possible for someone that age to pass away from an undiagnosed problem," the chief pointed out. "We will, however, be looking into the man's death for the cause."

"Are we in danger?" Mary demanded.

"There's no reason to believe you're in any danger," the chief said kindly. "We'll investigate closely to be certain this is an isolated incident."

Angie caught the chief's eye and gestured to the door. Chief Martin gave a quick nod to acknowledge Angie's and Finch's departure.

On the way to the car, Finch held Angie's arm as they made their way down the front steps of the beautiful, old house.

"There's a lot going on here, Miss Angie," Finch said. "I think we'll have our work cut out for us."

As she opened the passenger side door for Mr. Finch, the young woman took a quick glance back to the house and shuddered. "You can say that again."

3

"Chief Martin will be asking all of us to investigate." Standing in the large kitchen of the Victorian mansion she'd inherited from a distant relative, Angie used a spatula to fold sour cream into the brownie mixture she was preparing.

"What do you think went on in that boarding house?" Ellie, the middle Roseland sister, had long blond hair and a slim build. She was the one family member who did not appreciate paranormal powers and wished their abilities would disappear, but she had used her telekinesis skills more than once to protect her sisters and Mr. Finch when trouble headed their way.

The two family cats sat on top of the refrigerator

listening to the women's conversation. Euclid, a huge orange Maine Coon, and Circe, a small black cat with a little patch of white on her chest, paid close attention to what the sisters were saying.

Angie cocked her head to the side. "Perry Wildwood did not die from natural causes. I'm sure about that, but I have no idea who had a hand in taking his life or why."

Ellie placed a variety of cookies onto the white platter for the bed and breakfast guests. "So he was murdered," she said with resignation. "What happened? The killer snuck into the house and attacked the man while he slept?"

"That's possible." Angie slipped a baking pan into the oven. "It could also have been someone who was inside the house as a guest or a friend visiting someone he or she knew."

"Or maybe it was someone who lived there," Ellie suggested with narrowed eyes. "Does Maribeth keep track of people coming and going?"

"I don't think so." Angie gave a quick shrug.

"This will be difficult then." Ellie put a few strawberries around the cookie platter to give it a nice appearance. "When you and Mr. Finch spoke briefly with the residents, did you get an idea what Perry was like?"

"Very superficially." Angie mixed together ingredients for the chocolate frosting. "They all seemed to like him."

Courtney came into the kitchen through the back door of the Victorian. "Hi, all. What's cookin'?" Of the four siblings, the youngest Roseland sister resembled Angie the most with her honey-blond hair and blue eyes.

"Plenty," Angie said.

Courtney poured cereal into a bowl and added some milk before taking her snack to the kitchen island and sitting down. "Yeah? Like what?" she asked wiping some drops of milk from her lip.

"Someone died at the boarding house," Ellie said before heading for the dining room to put out the cookies.

"I heard people talking about that when I was working at the candy store." Courtney chuckled as she lifted her spoon to her lips. "Some people said someone was murdered there."

"Why are you laughing about that?" Ellie asked before stepping into the hallway.

"Because the idea is silly. Who'd get murdered at Maribeth's boarding house?" Courtney asked. "I thought it might have been an elderly resident who passed away and the tourists were being dramatic turning it into a murder."

"Angie will tell you about it." Ellie left the kitchen.

Courtney swallowed her spoonful of cereal and looked to her sister. "Tell me what? Wait. *Did* someone get murdered at the boarding house?"

"It seems someone did." Angie gave a nod and told Courtney what had transpired when she and Finch were making deliveries that morning.

"Mr. Finch was with you? I haven't seen him today. It was his day off." Courtney and Finch owned a popular candy shop located in the center of Sweet Cove. "It was a young guy who died? Did someone shoot him?"

"There wasn't any blood on the body that I could see. I think he was dead for a least a couple of hours," Angie said.

"Drug overdose?" Courtney questioned.

"Possibly."

"Could it have been intentional? Did the med student take his own life?"

"It's not the feeling I get." Angie removed a frying pan from the cabinet.

"What else do you know about the man?" Courtney asked.

"He was a second-year medical school student. The people in the house claimed he was well-liked. His name was Perry Wildwood. No brothers or sisters. His parents are dead. He was from Maine." Angie washed vegetables in the sink and then began to chop and dice them. "That's all I know."

"Girlfriend?" Courtney asked.

"No. The residents said he was too busy right now to get involved in a relationship," Angie told her sister.

"I wonder," Courtney thought over the facts. "He may have dated or had a fling with someone at school or maybe with someone he met in a bar. The person may not have liked Perry's noncommittal ways."

Angie looked over. "And then what? Killed him because Perry didn't have time to invest in a relationship?"

"Sure. There are a lot of nuts out there."

Euclid let out a loud hiss.

Courtney got up to make tea. "See. Euclid agrees with me."

Jenna, Angie's fraternal twin sister, came into the kitchen. Because she was taller than Angie and had long, dark brown hair, it often took some convincing to persuade people that the two really were twins. "What does Euclid agree with?"

Courtney put the kettle on the stove. "He agrees that someone could kill another person without having a good reason."

Jenna looked from one sister to the other. "Have I missed something? Did something happen?"

"A young man boarding at Maribeth's house got killed last night." Courtney set some mugs on the counter.

"Killed? Who was it? Who did it?" Jenna went to the stove to help Angie make dinner.

Angie and Courtney took turns relaying the information.

"We don't know much," Angie said.

"Chief Martin wants us to help with the case?" Jenna asked.

"He does," Courtney said with a delighted tone. "I was wondering when the next case would come along."

"I was hoping we could take the summer off from investigating." Angie stirred the simmering tomato sauce.

"If we do that, then we'll get rusty. We need to keep our skills sharp," Courtney said.

"We had a case just a month ago," Angie

protested. "We could have a few months off in between crimes and still maintain our abilities."

"Well, duty calls." Courtney poured the hot water into the mugs. "And when it calls, we have to answer."

Angie let out a sigh. "It's just that there's a lot going on right now. These cases take a lot of energy."

"We'll pace ourselves." Jenna patted her twin on the back. "Tom's coming for dinner. He's finishing up for the day and then he'll head over." Jenna and Tom, who owned a construction and rehab company, had been married for just over a year and lived in a big, old house two doors down from the Victorian.

Mr. Finch came in from the back door. "Look who I found outside."

Josh Williams, Angie's husband of one month, spotted her at the stove and hurried over. Wrapping her in his arms, he gave her a sweet kiss. They'd been texting all day about what Angie and Finch had discovered at the boarding house.

"Is there anything new?" Josh asked.

"Nothing yet. Chief Martin will let us know as soon as he hears word from the medical examiner." Angie covered the big pot to let the sauce continue to simmer.

"I assume the chief will bring all of you into the investigation," Josh said.

"From the sound of things," Courtney told her brother-in-law, "Chief Martin will be needing our help."

Josh, tall, with sandy-colored hair and an athletic build, owned the Sweet Cove Resort and Hotel and he and his brother were business partners running a real estate development company. "The chief is lucky to have your assistance."

Circe arched her back in a long stretch and then she and Euclid jumped down off the refrigerator to greet Mr. Finch and Josh. The men reached down to pat the felines whose purrs filled the air.

"Why don't the cats ever greet me that way?" Courtney asked.

"Don't feel bad," Jenna smiled. "They don't greet me either."

"They have a soft spot for Mr. Finch," Ellie said. "And Josh living here is still a novelty."

"You mean they don't have a soft spot for me like they do for Mr. Finch?" Josh made a mock sad face.

"Sorry." Angie put her arm around her husband's waist. "There's only one Mr. Finch."

"Well, maybe I can come in second place," Josh hoped.

Circe looked up at Josh and trilled.

The family sat down at the big, glossy, wooden table in the dining room off the foyer to enjoy the dinner of lasagna, homemade meatballs, salad, and garlic bread. Angie noticed that an extra place setting had been added to the table, but she didn't ask Ellie why.

"I'm going to meet with the museum director in a few days to go over what needs to be done to put a second location of the bake shop in the museum," Angie told the group. "I did tell him I'm not convinced it's the best thing for me to do right now, but he talked me into a meeting."

"I think he's going to talk you into it," Courtney said.

"I think it's a wonderful idea," Finch said, "but it has to work for Miss Angie and her future plans."

"I don't want to dilute the brand," Angie said. "I'm not sure it's the right move."

Tom sipped from his glass of wine. "I think it will only strengthen your brand. It will bring the bake shop to the attention of people who don't come into town much. It will build the business and give it more exposure."

Angie listened to the family's opinions and promised to give it serious thought.

Ellie passed the bread basket to Mr. Finch. "What time did you say Chief Martin was coming by?"

While everyone gave Ellie a sideways look, the cats stared down at her from their perch on top of the tall hutch. Ellie often had the feeling that someone was on the way to the house before that person showed up.

"I didn't say," Angie told her sister. "He's waiting for the results from the medical examiner. I don't know when he'll have the information for us."

Before anyone else could say something, and as if right on cue, the doorbell rang.

4

"Sorry I didn't call first. I was coming by this way and decided to see if you were at home." Chief Martin stood on the front porch.

"It's fine," Courtney said with a smile. "We're just sitting down to dinner. Come and join us. Ellie set a place for you."

The chief stepped into the foyer. "Did she? How did she know I was ....?" He let his sentence trail off. "Oh. Right."

The family greeted the man warmly, the cats trilled at him, he took a seat, and Courtney passed the food over.

"Smells delicious. As always." The chief placed a hearty square of lasagna on his plate. "Lucille is out with friends this evening so I was on my own for dinner. I appreciate the meal."

Mr. Finch asked, "You have news, Phillip?"

"I do. Shall I wait until after we've eaten?"

"It's okay," Angie told the chief. "We don't need to wait."

After clearing his throat, Chief Martin said, "The testing was done very quickly. We called in a favor in order to get the work done. It seems Perry Wildwood had antihistamines in his system. He also had a fatal dose of melathiocaine in his bloodstream. The medical examiner reported that it would have been administered by injection."

"It was an overdose?" Jenna blinked.

"It was definitely an overdose."

"Perry was a medical student," Ellie observed. "He would probably have access to medications and substances. He injected himself then?"

"That question has not been settled," the chief said. "The amount of melathiocaine was such that it would only have taken seconds to render the man unconscious. The medical examiner believes in such a case, the needle and syringe would still be in place in the arm, or at the very least, would have fallen to the floor if it had been self-injected."

"The syringe wasn't found?" Courtney asked.

"I didn't see one when I was there," Angie told the family.

"A search of the room did not turn up a syringe," Chief Martin said.

"So Perry Wildwood did not self-medicate?" Josh asked. "Someone else administered the drug?"

"So it seems." The chief gave a nod.

Euclid let out a low hiss.

"What is melathiocaine used for?" Tom questioned.

"Topical melathiocaine is rubbed on the skin to numb the area in cases of poison ivy, a burn, a cut or scratch, or insect bites." The chief took a swallow from his glass and continued. "An injection of melathiocaine works to reduce pain for an invasive procedure like surgery, needle puncture, putting in a breathing tube. It is sometimes used for relief of headaches or migraines."

Finch asked, "Do you think Mr. Wildwood may have had a migraine, someone tried to help by injecting the melathiocaine, and the young man had a fatal reaction to the drug?"

"It's certainly a possibility. A friend or acquaintance may have tried to help with the headache by administering the injection, then panicked when Perry fell unconscious," the chief said.

Ellie scowled. "If someone you knew had a serious reaction to something, wouldn't you call an ambulance?"

"Yes, but if it was another medical student or someone studying in a field of medical support, that person might lose their license to practice ... or may never be allowed a license to work," the chief said.

"There are two other people living in the boarding house who are students in medical professions," Angie said. "Megan Milton is a pharmacy student and Andy Hobbs is a student nurse."

"Oh," Jenna said with wide eyes. "Maybe one of them tried to help Perry and when Perry had the bad reaction, he or she took off with the syringe and anything else that might point to what had happened."

"Time for some conversations with the people in the house," Courtney said.

"Exactly," The chief agreed.

"Do you know any more about the young man?" Finch asked. "Friends? Dates? What he did in his spare time?"

"We don't know much yet. Only what you know already." The chief outlined the information they had so the others would be brought up to speed. "Single, didn't date much, no siblings, parents are gone, only a mention of a distant uncle, grew up in Maine. Perry was described as likeable, kind, helpful, nice to be around. The people in the boarding house liked him. That's all that's been found out so far. An officer was sent to find and speak with the medical students who knew him."

"Let's consider that Perry *did* inject himself," Angie suggested. "What could have happened to the syringe?"

The family members thought for a moment.

Jenna said, "Someone might have entered Perry's room, found him unresponsive, saw the syringe, and took it away."

"Why though?" Tom asked.

"The person could have assumed Perry committed suicide and did not want people to know what he'd done." Jenna gave a shrug.

"So that person would have found Perry after he died," Ellie said. "Taking away the syringe wouldn't result in any criminal charges, would it?"

"The circumstances surrounding the removal would have to be considered," the chief said.

"Is there another reason someone may have removed the syringe?" Angie asked.

Courtney said, "The person may have worried the police would think he or she gave the injection and wanted to avoid being investigated as a suspect in a murder."

"Why would the person think he'd become a suspect?" Jenna asked. "What could he have done that would make him worried about such a thing?"

"Mr. Wildwood and the person may have gotten into an argument or a fight," Finch said. "There may have been witnesses to their disagreement."

"Or the person might have had feelings for Perry that weren't reciprocated," Ellie said. "The feelings might have been obsessive. The person might have been overly attentive to Perry trying to change his mind, maybe the person stalked him. Others might know about this behavior and might accuse the person of killing Perry because he didn't return the feelings." Ellie held her hands up in a helpless gesture. "It's outlandish, sure, but it's happened."

Courtney nodded. "Mr. Finch and I have seen several true crime shows dealing with that exact situation."

"Gosh. This could be a very tangled web that we have on our hands," Jenna said.

The family processed the information while the table was cleared and the raspberry cooler cake and the coffee were brought out.

When everyone was settled around the table

again, Angie asked the chief, "How would you like us to begin? Where should we start?"

"I'd like two of you to go to the boarding house to speak with Maribeth. As you can imagine, she's very upset. She needed a little medication for the anxiety. I talked to her late this afternoon and she seems to be holding up. If you could start by speaking with her, I think it would be a good beginning. She might have some insight into Perry's mood and mindset. She might be familiar with his visitors. She could suggest who you might talk to about him, friends, people he may have dated."

"What about Megan Milton and Andy Hobbs? Should we speak with them?" Angie asked.

"Definitely," the chief said. "They might know quite a lot about Perry. Whether or not they'll share that information is yet to be seen. And of course, one of them may have helped administer the injection and will try to steer you in a different direction. You know the drill. Keep on your toes around these people. Watch their body language. Nonverbal communication is often more telling than actual words."

When Euclid made a grumbling sound deep in his throat, Chief Martin looked up at the cat and then said, "And remember to pay attention to tone of voice."

"Don't worry," Courtney said with a wink. "We're experts by now. And if we can't help you crack this case, there are two clever felines who will step in."

"I've no doubt." The chief gave the cats an appreciative nod.

"What about the other two boarding house residents?" Finch asked. "Mary Bishop and Roger Winthrop. I assume they're most often at home in the house?"

"Mrs. Bishop has a part-time job at a doctor's office. She works two or three days a week," the chief said. "She's also very social and meets friends every day. Mr. Winthrop does some tutoring at the house and writes science textbooks, but he sometimes works from the house when he's writing so he's at home most of the time," the chief said. "Their insights could prove to be very helpful. You can add them to the list of people to talk with."

"Would anyone like to go with me tomorrow?" Angie asked. "I have to make a delivery to the boarding house anyway so it would be a good time to speak to Maribeth."

Finch said, "I might be more helpful when you talk to Ms. Bishop and Mr. Winthrop. Being an older person, I might better connect with those two. Perhaps, I'll wait and accompany you when you meet with them."

"That's a great idea, Mr. Finch," Angie agreed.

"I'll go tomorrow," Courtney told her sister. "I like Maribeth. I already have a rapport with her. I think she's a character. She comes into the candy store a lot and we have good conversations."

"Perfect," Angie said.

Only half-kidding, Courtney narrowed her eyes and warned the family, "When you're in that house, be super careful around everyone. It wouldn't take much to sidle up to someone and stick them with a syringe of melathiocaine. We don't want to be anyone's next victim."

Her sister's words caused Angie's stomach to drop like a stone as cold sweat ran down her back.

5

I t was late afternoon when Angie and the bake shop's assistant manager, Louisa, walked up to the door of the Sweet Cove Museum. Located a few blocks from the shops and restaurants of Coveside at the southern end of town, the museum was one of the finest of its size in the country. It housed collections of American art, photography, maritime art, Native American art, and Asian art, as well as an expansive collection of textiles. A soaring glass roof covered the atrium at the middle of the museum with four brick buildings radiating out from the center. The open light-filled space led visitors into the galleries and studios.

"I've always loved this place," Louisa said. In her late twenties, the young woman had lovely skin and long black hair with the ends tinged blue. Having been a dancer since she was a little girl, no matter what she was doing, Louisa's movements were fluid and graceful. "I used to come with my mother and grandmother to see the galleries."

"It's a beautiful museum." Angie opened the door and entered into the welcoming foyer that led into the airy atrium. The museum director, Wilton Rutherford, sixty years old, athletic, and well-dressed, stood to the side speaking with a woman and when he spotted Angie and Louisa, he and the woman hurried over to greet them.

"This is Bonnie Most a member of the board of directors. You don't have any idea how much we love your bake shop," Wilton said. "It would make a perfect addition to the museum." Wilton and Bonnie led the two young women to a corner of the atrium. "We envision tables and chairs here with potted trees and with rectangular planters here and here," the Bonnie gestured. "The planters would be filled with seasonal flowers, greenery, and decorations.

Milton moved a few yards to the right. "Over this way, we'll build the kitchen area to your specifications. A bake shop cafe would be a very attractive addition to the museum and a lovely benefit for the visitors to have such delicious bakery items, coffees and teas, breads, soups, salads, and sandwiches available throughout the day."

"What do you think of the space?" Bonnie asked.

"I think it's very nice," Angie said. "Very bright and open."

"Come to the office suites. We have some tentative plans to show you." Milton led the way through one of the galleries to the management offices and into a sitting room decorated with early nineteenth-century furniture. Large glass windows looked out over the beautifully landscaped gardens.

Angie and Louisa admired the room and then took seats at the wooden table where computer-drawn images of the new museum bake shop café rested across the surface. Bonnie and Milton explained the layout and then showed renderings of the envisioned café and kitchen within the atrium.

Louisa couldn't help letting out an *ooh* when she saw the pictures. "This is gorgeous. What do you think, Angie?"

"The space is great, really lovely." When Angie leaned over the designs, her hair fell forward and she pushed the strands back behind her ears. "Do you have copies of the plans? I'd like to show them to my family. My husband is a real estate developer and owner of the Sweet Cove resort and my brother-in-law owns a renovation and construction company. I'd like their opinions and I'd like to review the plans with my sisters and a family friend."

"Of course," Milton said. "We have copies in a folder for you to take along with you."

"What's your initial impression?" Bonnie asked. "Is this something you think you'd like to pursue further?"

"I would." Angie nodded. "I've had expansion in the back of my mind for some time. I didn't think it would happen so quickly though. It's taken me by surprise and I need to give it a good deal of thought, but it seems like a very good opportunity."

Wilton opened an armoire to reveal a coffee bar and he took out glass cups and mugs. "How about a cappuccino or a latte?" When the women agreed, the man began to work the machine. "I have a smaller version at home. I love coffee."

Bonnie carried the first two beverages over to Angie and Louisa. "Have you heard the news about the boarding house? A possible homicide took place there."

Angie was surprised that Bonnie brought up the case and wasn't sure she wanted to share with the board member or the museum director that she was there shortly after the body had been found. "We heard, yes. Terrible."

"Such a young person," Louisa said. "Maybe it wasn't a murder. Maybe he had an undiagnosed heart defect or some other physical problem."

Bonnie sat across the table with her cup. "I wonder. It would be ironic wouldn't it? If the man was in medical school and he had a defect that was never discovered by a health professional." The woman sipped from her mug.

"I met Perry Wildwood once at a charity event," Wilton said as he sat down with his mug of coffee. "He was the president of the medical school student association. We had a long conversation. I was impressed with him, very intelligent, yet he had an easy way about him. Very approachable and a winning personality. A real shame. A terrible loss. I think he would have gone on to do great things. He had a strong interest in neurological issues. He told me he suffered from excruciating migraines."

Angie's senses perked up. "Did he? Did he tell you how he handled them?"

"Perry said he'd tried everything to no avail. He mentioned he'd hoped to become a surgeon, but that specialty would be impossible due to the frequent, incapacitating headaches."

"Did he talk about treating himself? Trying different remedies himself?" Angie asked.

"He didn't go into such detail," Wilton said. "I remember he'd said he'd been to many different doctors. Nothing helped."

Bonnie spoke up. "My brother is a doctor. I believe it is frowned upon for doctors to self-prescribe medications and they definitely can't prescribe controlled substances for themselves. A medical student certainly wouldn't be able to do such a thing."

"Did Perry talk about how his migraines impacted his studies? Was he able to keep up with classes and rotations?" Angie asked.

"He didn't say much about that other than to mention it had been difficult to manage the work with the migraines," Wilton said. "I never realized the disabling nature of severe headaches. Anyway, the young man's passing is a real loss."

"Do the police think Perry was murdered?" Louisa asked.

"I believe the investigation is on-going," Angie said.

"I like the idea of living in a boarding house," Bonnie said. "If you're a student or young professional or someone who doesn't have relatives around, you have the benefit of interacting with other people, different ages in a quiet, family-type atmosphere. It seems healthier than living in a dorm surrounded by same-age people who are probably stressed out a lot of the time. I've met the owner of the boarding house. Maribeth Perkins, a very pleasant woman."

Angie's eyes widened. "Where did you meet?"

"We were taking a gardening course together. It was held at the horticultural hall," Bonnie said. "We got to talking. She was very attached to the residents of her home. I loved the idea of bringing back the boarding house. Maribeth's place is always full so there must be a niche to fill."

"Maribeth contracts with me to provide baked goods for her house," Angie said.

"So you know her," Bonnie said. "How is she holding up? She must have been horrified that the young man was found dead in her house."

"She was quite distraught, of course," Angie said. "But I've heard she's doing better. I'll see her tomorrow."

"Please give her my regards," Bonnie said.

"I can't imagine how Perry's girlfriend is managing," Wilton said with a sad shake of the head.

"Perry had a girlfriend?" Angie asked. "I'd heard he wasn't in a relationship."

"When I met Perry at the charity ball, he had a woman with him. He introduced her to me as his girlfriend. Perhaps they'd broken up?"

"I don't know," Angie said. "Do you remember the woman's name?"

Wilton tapped his chin with his forefinger. "Let me see. I'm usually good at names. Hmm. Oh, yes. Maura. That was her name."

"Do you remember her last name?"

"I don't recall hearing the last name."

"What did she look like?" Angie asked.

"Very attractive. Short hair, almost cut like a boy, elfish. Blue eyes. Slim. Not tall, average height," Wilton said.

"Do you know where she lived?"

"Near the medical school and the hospital," Wilton said. "Maura told me she'd love to have a room at the boarding house, but the place was full. She complained about her studio apartment being in a very noisy building."

"Was she a medical student?" Angie questioned.

"She was. I think she was ahead of Perry in school. She told me she was going into anesthesiology."

"A demanding field," Angie said.

"She seemed like a nice person. She seemed to dote on Perry," Wilton said. "Poor woman. I hope she's doing okay."

Angie was amazed that her business meeting at the museum had provided such unexpected information. Perry had severe migraines and not much had helped him despite getting the advice of several doctors. Perry had dated a med school student named Maura. Bonnie had met Maribeth at a gardening class and had the impression that the woman was very pleasant and was devoted to the boarding house occupants.

Who was Maura? Was Perry still dating her or had they broken up? Maura was studying anesthesiology. She would have access to drugs. Did she try to help Perry's migraine by injecting him with melathiocaine? Was Perry's death an accident? Or could Maura have given him an intentional overdose? Had he broken up with her? Was she so angry about it that she killed the man?

Thinking everything over, Angie's hand shook with apprehension when she reached for her cup.

Time to find Maura.

6

"I'm doing much better." Maribeth's hand shook as she brushed at her cheek. "I have my routine and that distracts me some." The woman glanced out at the hallway from her small office where she, Angie, and Courtney sat in comfortable chairs near the window. The room had rich wood paneling and a wall covered with shelves filled from top to bottom with books. "I wish the police would figure out what happened to poor Perry. I can't get it out of my mind." Leaning forward, Maribeth lowered her voice. "What if someone deliberately hurt Perry? Have I met the person who did it? Do I still run into him?" She let out a long, sad breath. "The idea makes my skin crawl."

"The police will get to the bottom of it."

Courtney gave the woman a reassuring smile. "Then you won't have to think about it anymore."

"That will be a blessing." Maribeth shook her head. "I know I'll rally. I just need more time to process the whole thing, then I'll be able to handle it better. All my life, I've been able to pick myself up after setbacks ... and I've had plenty of them. You have to take the bitter with the sweet. That's what life is like. You can't let the bad things pull you under. You have to push through and keep going. You can't give up."

"You have a very good attitude," Angie told her. "But you need to give yourself time. It's normal to feel strongly about such a terrible thing, to be upset by it, to feel loss."

"To be suspicious about people?" Maribeth asked.

"Yes. To feel suspicious, to wonder what happened to Perry, to ask why."

"I just want it be over so things can go back to normal." Maribeth pressed two fingers against her temple. "The investigators come around, they ask questions. The residents get worried, concerned. I don't want them to move out. I need the income that the leases bring in. What if everyone moves away and no one will rent from me again? And besides, I'd miss everyone if they left me and moved somewhere else."

"I don't think you need to worry about that. You have people here who plan to stay for the long term," Angie said. "Some of the people consider this their home."

"I hope you're right." Maribeth slowly shook her head and looked out the window to the backyard gardens.

Angie asked gently. "Did you see Perry the day he passed away?"

Maribeth blinked a few times. "He had breakfast early like he usually does. He ate in the kitchen while I was working. Perry left for the hospital for a meeting and a lecture and I didn't see him until later. He was working in his room, sitting at his desk. I know because he had his door open and I went past a couple of times."

"Did he have dinner here?" Courtney questioned.

"We only have dinner as a household on Wednesdays," Maribeth said. "Every other evening, the residents fend for themselves. Sometimes, a resident will make a big lasagna or a pot of stew or chili and he or she shares the meal with whoever is around."

"Did you see Perry in the house when it was dinnertime?" Courtney restated her question. "Did he cook something for himself? Did he go out maybe?"

"Perry ordered takeout food. I went to the door when it rang. It was the delivery person. Perry came out and paid the young man and took his food into the kitchen."

"Were you in the kitchen when Perry was eating?" Angie asked.

"I was in and out. I made a cup of tea and we chatted while I was waiting for the water to boil," Maribeth said.

"How was Perry's mood?" Courtney asked.

Maribeth leaned against the chair back. "He was his usual pleasant self. It was general chit chat."

"So it didn't seem like anything was bothering him?"

"No. At least I didn't notice. I wasn't in the kitchen for any length of time."

"What was Perry eating?" Angie asked.

"Eating? I don't really remember. Why do you ask?"

"I wondered where he'd ordered the food from."

"Let's see." Maribeth rubbed the bottom of her chin as she thought. "I didn't recognize the delivery man. I didn't notice what he was driving so I didn't see a business name on the vehicle. I can't say what Perry bought for dinner. I don't recall what he was eating that night."

"What did Perry do after he finished his dinner?" Courtney asked.

"He cleaned up the dishes and returned to his room," Maribeth said.

"Did you see him again that evening?" Angie questioned.

"No, I didn't. At least not to speak with. I passed him as he was going to the kitchen."

"Did he have a guest or a visitor after dinner?" Courtney rested her elbow on the arm of her chair.

"I remembered hearing voices in his room," Maribeth said. "A man, I believe, but I didn't see him."

"Did you recognize the voice?" Angie asked.

"I just don't know," Maribeth said. "The police asked the same question of me, but I can't answer it. Maybe it was Andy, the nursing student who lives here, but I can't be certain. It was a young man's voice though, that I'm sure of."

"Was Megan around that evening?" Courtney asked.

"Yes, she read in the den for a while with Roger

Winthrop and Mary Bishop. The three of them are bookworms. They always have their noses in a story."

"Did Megan, Mary, or Roger seem bothered by anything?" Angie asked. "Did either of them seem out of sorts, angry about anything?"

Maribeth said, "Roger can be cantankerous, but he's a kind man. It's just how he is. He means well. Someone else might interact with Roger and claim he was out of sorts, but you have to know him. As far as I could see, the three of them were their normal selves."

"What were you doing that evening?" Courtney asked.

Maribeth gave an account of her night. "I worked here in my office for some time, and then I went to the den and made a fire for the bookworms. I sat in there reading with them for about an hour, then I returned to the kitchen to make some batter for the morning waffles. Mary Bishop left the den with me and said she wanted to turn in early so we wished each other goodnight and went our separate ways."

Courtney asked another question. "Did you hear anything unusual during the evening or the night? An argument? A complaint? The sounds of a person who was annoyed with someone else?"

"I didn't hear anything like that."

"When did you go to bed?" Angie asked.

"I went up to my rooms sometime after 11pm," Maribeth said.

"Your rooms are on the second floor?"

"Yes, they are. There are a total of seven bedroom suites in the house, the residents occupy four bedrooms upstairs and two downstairs. I occupy the fifth bedroom suite on the second floor."

"Who had rooms on the first floor?" Courtney questioned.

"Perry had one and Megan had the other. The older residents living in the house right now prefer the second floor because they think it's quieter up there away from the common rooms and the kitchen. There's a small elevator near the backdoor of the house so the stairs aren't of concern to them."

"Have you talked to Megan about the night Perry died?"

Maribeth seemed to shrink in her chair. "A little."

"Did Megan hear anything unusual that night?" Angie asked.

"No." Maribeth looked at Angie. "She only heard us in the morning when I brought you and Mr. Finch inside. Megan was sleeping later than usual.

She heard the commotion and came to see what was going on."

"Were Megan and Perry friends?" Courtney asked.

"I would say so. They had busy schedules, but sometimes they'd cook dinner together or study together in each other's room," Maribeth told the young women.

Angie asked, "Did Perry have any health problems?"

"Health problems?" Maribeth's forehead scrunched up. "No, but he did have bad headaches."

"Frequently?"

"Often. He told me they ran in his family. He suffered when they came on."

"Did medication help him?"

"He said he'd never really found any medication that helped. He did yoga, ran, saw a chiropractor, was careful about what he ate, hardly drank any alcohol at all." Maribeth shook her head. "He'd close his door, put in ear plugs to block out any noise, and pull the shades to keep the light out. The headaches would last hours ... sometimes they went on for nearly two days." The woman lowered her voice and leaned slightly forward. "Megan mentioned to me that Perry's father once attempted suicide because of his own terrible headaches."

"Oh, gosh." Courtney's face took on an expression of horror. "The poor man."

"Most people have difficult things to bear," Maribeth said. "My husband died when he was only fifty. A sudden heart attack." She sighed. "And my son, my only child, died in a car accident when he was seventeen. I had a hard time coping with those two losses. I couldn't sleep, I could hardy eat. My work suffered. When my uncle passed away and left this house to me, it was the chance for a new start. I quit my job and turned this place into a boarding house. I like having people around. I enjoy providing a safe, cozy, comfortable home for people. Things have been going so well ... until Perry...." She let her voice trail off. "I hope the police find out soon what happened to him. My mind runs away with ideas sometimes. I worry that someone might have killed him."

"The Sweet Cove police have an excellent record for solving serious crimes," Courtney said. "They have one of the best records on the entire east coast."

"That's encouraging," Maribeth said.

Angie wanted to talk about something less distressing to Maribeth so she asked, "What did you do for work before you starting running the boarding house?"

"I was a registered nurse. I studied nursing and got my bachelor's and master's degrees. The job was very stressful. It was the right time for me to leave. I'm forever thankful to my uncle for leaving me this house. Good things do happen. We all have to focus on our blessings."

Yes, Angie thought. *I'm grateful for my family every day.*

But sometimes, one's focus has to be placed on other things.

7

Courtney and Angie left the boarding house and were heading to their car when a woman's voice called to them. Megan Milton was getting out of her parked car when she spotted the sisters on the walkway.

Angie introduced Courtney to the young pharmacy student.

"How are you doing?" Megan asked Angie.

"Okay. We made a delivery to the house and brought some flowers for Maribeth to let her know we're thinking of her."

"That was nice of you," Megan said with a nod of her head. "Have you heard anything from the police? Do they know what happened to Perry?"

"I think they're still investigating," Angie said not

wanting to reveal that Police Chief Martin had shared some information with them.

Megan gestured to two benches under a shade tree. "Can you sit for a few minutes?"

Angie and Courtney exchanged a look of agreement.

"Sure. We have some time before we need to get back to work," Angie told her.

The early morning air was warming quickly promising an unusually hot day, but it was pleasantly cool under the tall, leafy tree.

When they were sitting on the benches, Megan said, "It can be hard living in the house. I had the room across from Perry's. I know he most likely died of an accidental overdose, but late at night, I start to worry. I'm afraid someone might have killed him. I can't turn my mind off and I have a hard time sleeping."

"It's understandable," Courtney said. "It's a traumatic event. You were friendly with Perry."

"How could someone get into the house?" Megan asked. "Maribeth keeps everything in good working order. The locks are up-to-date. You have to use a key to get inside. There wasn't any sign of a break-in. The police told me that. Then how did someone get in?"

"Maybe no one *did* get in," Angie said. "Like you said, Perry probably died of an accidental overdose."

"Do you think he did?" Megan looked straight at Angie.

"It's a possibility," Angie replied.

"Perry was only twenty-five. Most people his age don't pass away."

"It happens though," Courtney said. "He may have had a health issue that he was unaware of."

Megan rubbed at the back of her neck. "I don't know. He had those headaches, but otherwise, he seemed healthy and fit. Wouldn't a health issue have shown up in some way by his age?"

"I don't really know," Courtney told her, "but the medical examiner will be able to figure out what the cause of death was."

"Do you think he might have had a stroke?" Megan asked. "Could his migraines have caused a stroke?"

"Did Perry have a migraine that day?" Angie asked.

"When I saw him in the afternoon, he complained to me that he felt off. Sometimes when a headache was coming on, he would say he felt off in the head. Other times he felt sick to his stomach right before a headache hit."

"You saw him in the afternoon?" Courtney questioned.

"Yeah. He came home a little earlier than usual. I asked him if he wanted to study together later in the evening. He told me he wasn't sure because he wasn't feeling great. He said he'd see how things went."

"Did you end up getting together to study?" Angie asked.

Megan said, "He and I had some pasta and bread for dinner in the kitchen. Perry had ordered it from a take-out place. After we ate, he told me he was going to sleep for a while and if he felt better, he'd come by my room. I read in the den for an hour, and then I decided to go out for a while so I texted him that I wouldn't be around. He didn't answer, but my text didn't need an answer."

"Did you study together a lot?" Courtney asked.

"A couple of times a week."

"Did Andy Hobbs study with the two of you?"

"No. I asked him, but he never joined us. I think Andy liked to study on his own and anyway...." Megan gave a shrug.

Angie heard something in the young woman's voice. "What were you going to say?" she asked.

"Andy didn't seem to like Perry all that much. I

kind of thought Andy had a chip on his shoulder when he was around Perry."

"Why would he?" Courtney turned a little on the bench to better see Megan's face.

"I don't know. I think Andy resented that Perry was in medical school and he wasn't."

"He could have applied to med school," Courtney said.

"He did apply. He didn't get in."

"Did Perry and Andy avoid each other?" Angie asked.

"Perry was friendly, but Andy didn't reciprocate. He stayed to himself a lot. Maybe it was the age difference between Andy and us."

"Is Andy that much older?"

"Not really. He's ten years older, but it seems to make a difference to him. He's been married and divorced and is changing careers so I think he feels a lot more mature than he thinks we are." Megan shrugged. "I'm just guessing. Andy never said anything. It's just different personalities and people in different places in their lives."

Angie wondered if there was more to Andy disliking Perry than what Megan described.

"You said you went out after having dinner with

Perry the night he died," Angie said. "Where did you go?"

"I met a friend for a couple of drinks."

"Where did you go?"

"The Sweet Cove resort."

"Did you hear anything during the night?" Courtney asked. "Did anything wake you up?"

"I woke up a couple of times, but I don't think it was because of a noise or a disturbance. Whenever I drink, I often have a restless sleep," Megan said.

"So you don't think you woke up because of a noise?"

"I don't think so. When I was awake and falling back to sleep, I didn't notice any sounds in the house."

"Did you stay awake for very long each time you woke up?"

"No, I fell right back to sleep. I don't usually toss and turn. I just sleep lightly whenever I drink."

"Did you hear Perry talking to anyone?"

Something passed over Megan's face and her forehead lined in thought. "I don't think so. I don't remember hearing his voice."

"Did Perry have a girlfriend?" Angie asked.

"He was too busy. He told me it wasn't the time to make a commitment to someone."

"He had a girlfriend recently though?" Angie asked.

"When he first started school he did. He broke it off."

"Who was the girlfriend?" Courtney asked.

Megan said, "Her name is Maura Norris. She's doing her residency now. She was in her last year of school when Perry started."

"Where is she now?"

"She's doing her residency in Boston."

"Do you know Maura?" Angie asked.

"I met her a couple of times. She came here to the house right before they broke up."

"How was the break-up? Was it friendly?"

"Perry didn't talk about it much. He said Maura wasn't happy about it, but he just wasn't ready for a permanent relationship and that's what Maura wanted," Megan said.

Courtney used an even tone when she asked, "Did you and Perry have a relationship?"

Megan's cheeks turned pink. "Me? No. We were friends, that's all."

"Did you want to be more than friends?" Courtney questioned.

Even though Megan said no, the pink in her

cheeks brightened which seemed to contradict her negative response.

"Are you seeing anyone?" Angie asked.

"No. My boyfriend and I broke up right before I moved here for school. I have to be in pharmacy school for years and he didn't like the idea of being separated for so long. I had to agree with him."

"Did you have feelings for Perry?"

Megan swallowed and her eyes darted around the garden before saying softly, "We were friends." There was a long silence before she added, "I think Perry felt the same way. I knew he didn't want anything serious."

"Did *you* want something serious?"

Megan let out a long sigh and some moisture glistened at the edge of her eyes. "Perry was a great guy. We were similar in a lot of ways. We got along really well. Maybe if we met at another time in our lives, something would have happened. Honestly? I liked him, but I held back because I knew it wasn't something Perry wanted."

"Did you resent him?" Courtney asked.

"Of course not. Perry was clear about wanting to remain friends. It would have been stupid for me to fall for him."

"He told you he only wanted to be friends?" Angie asked.

"Not in so many words." Megan straightened up. "Perry talked a couple of times about why he broke up with Maura. It wouldn't be any different with another woman. Perry was putting his attention solely on reaching his goal of being a doctor. He didn't have the energy necessary for both his studies and a relationship." The young woman passed the back of her hand over her eyes. "Sure, I would have liked things to move beyond being friends, but it was never going to happen and I made sure to stay within the bounds of friendship."

"Did Perry know how you felt about him?" Angie questioned.

"I was very careful never to let on." Megan's lips were tight. "Anyway, I want to know what happened to Perry. Hasn't the medical examiner figured it out yet? What's taking so long to get an answer?"

"We'll probably hear very soon," Angie said.

"Well, I need to go inside and get ready for an exam." Megan stood up. "Thanks for chatting. I'll see you around."

As soon as Megan disappeared into the house, Courtney turned to her sister. "I get a weird feeling from Megan. Do you think she isn't being upfront with us? Is she keeping some things to herself?"

Angie ran her hands over her arms. Despite the morning's increasing temperature, goosebumps formed over her skin. "That's exactly what I've been wondering."

8

————

Sitting on a lounge chair under the pergola in the backyard of the Victorian, Euclid lifted his orange head to sniff at the delicious aromas floating on the air.

Wearing barbecue aprons, Josh and Tom stood near the fire pit grilling steak tips, vegetables, and eggplant cutlets and chatting with Angie and Mr. Finch about the case. Circe was curled on Finch's lap enjoying the man's petting.

"I think Megan knows more than she's saying." Angie put a clean platter on the stonewall next to the fire pit.

"Do you have an idea what she's holding back about?" Josh turned the steak tips with a large grilling fork.

"I don't. Courtney doesn't know either, but she got a feeling from Megan that she wasn't being upfront with us about something."

"What about Maribeth? Did you talk to her?" Josh asked.

"We did. I didn't realize the tragedies she's had to deal with over the years." Angie poured a drink of iced tea for Finch and then proceeded to tell the men about Maribeth losing her husband and son. "She's quite upset over Perry Wildwood, because of the man's death and because she's afraid she'll lose her livelihood should her residents decide to move away and no one else will lease from her."

"I don't think Maribeth needs to worry about that." Tom adjusted the grill's flames. "I don't think Perry's death would turn people off from living in the boarding house. It's an unfortunate event, but they can't blame Maribeth. I've heard she's very careful about security at the house, updating the locks and the windows and keeping everything in good working order. If someone broke in, then they must have broken a window or used a sophisticated tool to bust open the lock."

"Can somebody break a window without making noise?" Courtney carried over a tray of glasses and a pitcher of lemonade and set them on the side table near the grill.

"What if the person placed a couple of suction cups on the window and then used a glass cutter to cut it open," Josh said, "then reached inside the hole in the window and unlocked it?"

"That would work," Tom agreed. "The suction cups would keep the window from shattering. There wouldn't be any noise."

"So the break-in would have been planned," Finch said while running his hand over the black cat's fur. "And the plan probably included killing Perry, don't you think?"

"I think murdering Perry was the plan," Courtney said. "Perry had an overdose of melathiocaine in his system. No one just happens to carry around a syringe of melathiocaine with them. If someone broke into the boarding house, killing Perry was the reason."

"Have the police made a determination about a break-in?" Josh asked.

"We haven't heard." Angie sipped from her glass of iced tea mixed with lemonade.

Ellie came out through the backdoor carrying a green salad with tomatoes, onions, walnuts, and sliced strawberries and put it on the patio table. "You all look very serious. Are you discussing the case?"

Angie and Courtney brought their sister up-to-date with the latest news.

"I think it was someone who lives in the house." Ellie had a pair of shears in her back pocket and she removed them and went to the garden beside the carriage house to cut some flowers for a vase. Euclid followed her and sniffed the ground around the bottom of the huge tree.

"You think it was one of the residents who killed Perry?" Angie asked. "Why do you think that?"

"Nobody heard anything," Ellie explained. "That pharmacy student, what's her name? Megan, right? She has the room near Perry's, but she heard nothing that night. I don't think anyone broke in. I think the person was already in the house. Did Perry have a visitor that evening?"

"No one told us there was a visitor," Courtney said.

"That doesn't mean there wasn't one." Ellie snipped some blooms and slipped them into the white vase. "Perry made it clear he didn't want a relationship at that point in his life. He might have wanted an occasional one-night stand though."

Angie stared at her sister. "Huh. I didn't think of that."

"It didn't have to be a woman who dropped by to visit," Ellie said. "A friend of Perry's might have come by. People in the house might have been familiar with the friend so they paid no attention to the person being there. That could be the reason no one claims anything was unusual."

"Maybe you should be a detective," Angie said with a smile.

Ellie glanced over her shoulder at Angie and shook her head. "It's not rocket science. It's common sense stuff."

"But common sense stuff is often overlooked," Finch stated. "We all tend to ignore the ordinary or the familiar. Our brains go into autopilot which can make us miss the little things."

Euclid sat next to the garden swishing his tail, and then he leaned his head back and let out a loud, shrill howl.

Tom jumped slightly from the wildcat sound and almost dropped the tongs he was holding. "Gee, Euclid. Give me a warning when you're going to do that, will you?"

Jenna came down the back steps carrying an apple pie and she chuckled at Tom's startled reaction to the cat's noise. "I thought you'd be immune to Euclid's vocals by now."

"I'll never get used to that." Tom moved around the foil-wrapped ears of corn on the grill and shivered. "It's unworldly."

After putting the pie on the table, Jenna went up behind Tom, wrapped her arms around her husband's waist, and rested her cheek against his back.

"I'll never get used to this either," Tom smiled at his wife's attention. "It's heaven."

Courtney groaned. "No public displays of affection, please."

Jenna gave her sister a sly smile. "That can only happen when Rufus is here?"

Courtney ignored the comment about her boyfriend.

"Where is Rufus this evening, Miss Courtney?" Finch asked.

"He and Jack are working late today. They'll come by later. Ellie and I told them we'd put some food aside for them."

"I had lunch with Jack today." Ellie put the vase on the side table and fussed with arranging the flowers. "They picked up a new client and it's turned into more work than they expected." Jack, Ellie's boyfriend, owned a law firm in town and he and Rufus, a newly-minted attorney from England, worked together in a beautiful, grand, old building just off of Main Street.

Just as the group was sitting down to eat at the table under the pergola, Angie's phone buzzed with a text from Chief Martin. "The chief has something important to tell us. He asks if he can come by."

When everyone encouraged Angie to tell the man to come over for dinner, she sent the text and within ten minutes, Euclid and Circe padded over to the driveway to greet the chief.

"I'm always barging in on your meal." The chief walked across the lawn to the table.

"We're always glad to have you join us," Finch said. "Have a seat."

The serving bowls were passed over and Chief Martin filled the plate they'd set for him. Before digging in, he said, "I have some news about the Perry Wildwood case. Do you want to hear it now?"

"We can talk about it now. What have you found out?" Angie asked.

"Perry's laptop was taken from his room by investigators. We found something on it."

"Tell us." Courtney was eager to hear what had been discovered.

The chief cleared his throat. "A note."

The people around the table and the two cats on the lounge chairs were silent.

"It was written by Perry ... he talked about his struggles with the headaches. He wrote that it was difficult to go on, that he didn't think he'd be able to achieve his lifelong goal of becoming a doctor."

Ellie's hand moved to her throat. "A suicide note?"

Courtney's eyes narrowed. "No way. I don't believe it."

"Why don't you believe it?" Josh asked his sister-in-law.

"Becoming a doctor is what Perry wanted all of his life." Courtney's face was angry. "People reported that he was single-minded about becoming a physician. He worked hard. He took care of himself. He refused to become involved in a relationship until he finished his studies. Suicide doesn't fit."

"Sometimes people reach the end of their rope," Tom pointed out gently. "Sometimes, people give up."

Courtney's brow furrowed. "He deliberately injected himself with an overdose of medication?"

"It seems so," the chief said.

"Didn't the medical examiner mention that a

dosage that strong would have hit Perry like a ton of bricks?" Jenna asked.

"Not in so many words, but yes, he did." Chief Martin drank from his water glass.

"Didn't the medical examiner say the syringe might have remained in Perry's arm because the drug would have instantly put him out?" Jenna asked. "Or that it would have fallen to the floor?"

"Yes," the chief said.

"If that much medication was self-induced," Jenna said, "then where is the syringe?"

The chief said, "We discussed previously that someone might have found Perry, panicked, and hid the syringe either to keep themselves from falling under suspicion or to keep people from finding out Perry ended his own life." The chief looked from family member to family member. "Now there's a note that indicates Perry was under strain, was depressed, was feeling hopeless."

"No." Courtney folded her arms and leaned on the table. "I don't think so. Someone wants the world to believe that poor, sad Perry took his own life. That's not the impression I get of Perry. We can't fall for this. It's a trick."

"I think Courtney's right," Angie said.

Jenna chimed in with her thoughts. "Courtney

makes good points. I don't think we should take this at face value. We need to look into this before we accept that Perry wrote a suicide note."

The corners of the chief's mouth turned up a little. "I'm glad to hear you say this. It's what I think as well."

Ellie had been listening closely to the comments. Dabbing her lips with a napkin, she set it to the side of her plate and gave Mr. Finch a long look before turning to face the chief. "Can we see the note?"

"I can share it with you, yes," the chief said. "I have a paper copy of it in my briefcase."

"Can we see Perry's laptop? Can we see the note on the laptop?" Ellie asked. "Not a printed version."

"Sure. We can go down to the station whenever you like." A confused expression passed over the chief's face. "But why do you want to see the laptop?"

"Because," Ellie said, "Mr. Finch needs to touch the keyboard."

9

Mr. Victor Finch had the unusual ability to pick up information from people and objects simply by touching them. The only problem with his ability was that it could be unpredictable, sometimes strong, sometimes not working at all. No one understood the reason for the erratic nature of the skill and there didn't seem to be a way to control it, but when it worked, it could provide valuable clues to an investigation.

Finch took a seat at the scuffed old table in the police station's conference room and Angie sat on one side of the man and Courtney took the chair on the other side. The harsh brightness of the overhead fluorescent light burned Finch's eyes and he had to close them for a few moments.

"I see you've improved the lighting in this room," Finch kidded the chief.

"Should I turn off the lights for you? Would that help?" Chief Martin asked. "I could bring in the lamp from my office."

"It will be all right," Finch smiled and slowly opened his lids. "My eyes are adjusting."

Ellie leaned against the wall near the door and Jenna, holding Circe in her arms, stood next to her. Watching the proceedings with interest, Euclid sat on a wooden chair beside them.

Chief Martin left the room briefly and returned with a box. Inside was Perry's laptop. The chief placed the box on the table and then, wearing surgical-type gloves on his hands, he set the laptop in front of Finch. "Is there anything you need? Can I get you some water? Should the lights stay on or will they interfere with ... with what you do?"

"Thank you, Phillip," Finch said calmly as he slipped his hands into gloves provided to him by the chief. "Everything is fine. I'll begin now."

Everyone in the room went still as the older man closed his eyes again and slowly rested his fingertips on the keyboard of Perry's laptop.

Finch's face changed expression from serious to concerned over the several minutes that passed, and then he leaned back in his chair. "I am unable to pick up anything."

"Is it because of the gloves on your hands?" Angie asked. "Are they preventing you from feeling the sensations?"

"I don't believe the gloves should interfere," Finch said staring at the keyboard.

"Should we leave the room, Mr. Finch?" Courtney asked. "Is it distracting to have all of us with you?"

Finch patted the young woman's hand. "It is comforting to me to have all of you with me. Perhaps the sensations from the laptop have disappeared into the air or have been wiped away somehow."

Circe wiggled in Jenna's arms trying to get down so the young woman set the cat on the floor. The small, black feline darted to Mr. Finch and jumped onto his lap.

Surprised by the animal, Finch chuckled and patted her back as Circe put her front paws on the edge of the table and flicked her tail back and forth. The cat turned her head to Finch and then put her little paw on the keyboard.

"Try again, Mr. Finch," Courtney encouraged. "I think Circe wants you to give it another try."

"It can't hurt," Finch agreed. As soon as the older man said the words, the black cat contentedly settled on his lap.

Finch took in a long breath and closed his eyes and while his hand stroked the feline's fur, a look of calm came over his face. The family and Chief Martin waited and watched.

Finch's hand touched the keyboard and his fingers skimmed over the keys slowly moving from side to side. Ten minutes passed before Finch opened his eyes.

The man's facial muscles sagged showing signs of heavy fatigue and his shoulders slumped. He took in a long breath and removed his gloves. "I'm finished."

Circe placed her paws on the man's chest and licked his cheek while Chief Martin hurried in with a cup of water.

"No luck, Mr. Finch?" Courtney asked with a kind voice.

Finch sipped the cool water and cleared his throat. "On the contrary, this time I was able to pick up a few sensations."

"You were?" Angie said with excitement and she had to hold back from firing questions at the man.

"Much of what I picked up most likely belonged to the laptop's owner, Perry Wildwood. I was able to sense his ambition, his diligence and perseverance, and some of the pain he experienced from the migraines. I did not pick up any feelings of hopelessness."

"You didn't sense anything that indicated Perry had given up because of his headaches?" Jenna asked as she took a seat at the table.

"Nothing like that whatsoever." Finch smiled down at Circe who had settled again on his lap. "I also felt the sensation of two others when I touched the keys. One person who used the laptop seemed to have friendly feelings for Perry. I can't tease out if that person is a man or a woman. The second individual who used the keyboard did not convey feelings of friendship ... in fact, I picked up hostility from this person as well as anger, jealousy, and resentment. Again, I cannot tell if this individual is male or female."

Courtney wrapped her arms around the older man to give him a big hug. "Well done, Mr. Finch, well done."

"It's very good information," Angie nodded and

squeezed his shoulder. "It will help us as we move forward."

"I think my furry friend helped calm me so that I was able to feel the sensations." Finch scratched the cat's cheek. "Well done to you, too, little one."

Circe trilled as Ellie and Jenna came to Finch's side and gave him hugs.

Ellie asked the chief, "What about the suicide note that was found on this laptop? Can we see that now?"

With a nod, Chief Martin tapped on the keys and brought a document up on the screen. "Here it is." He stepped away so the others could cluster around to see what was written.

When everyone finished reading the letter, the room was silent for almost a full minute.

"Well," Jenna finally said, "it's a very sad telling of Perry's struggles."

"It's heartbreaking, really," Angie said.

"The headaches took a terrible toll on him," Ellie remarked with a long sigh.

Courtney's eyes narrowed and a look of disgust showed on her face. "I get the feeling this is a piece of fiction."

All eyes turned to the youngest Roseland sister.

"Do you?" the chief questioned.

"When Mr. Finch touched the keyboard, he didn't pick up a sense of hopelessness from Perry," Courtney said. "It seems to me that someone contemplating ending his life would feel hopeless."

"So you're implying that someone else wrote this letter?" Ellie asked.

"Yes, I am," Courtney said.

"Good," Ellie said, "because I feel the same way."

"Mr. Finch felt someone's anger and hostility when he was experiencing the keyboard," Angie pointed out. "That person might have killed Perry, and wrote this note."

"Do any of you think it's probable that Perry took his life?" Chief Martin asked.

No one responded.

"Okay then, we're all on the same page," the chief said with a nod. "Now the question is … who *did* end Perry's life?"

Angie looked up at the chief. "Could we go to the boarding house? Could we go and take a look at Perry's room again?"

Chief Martin didn't ask why. He simply nodded and said, "Let's go."

∼

PERRY'S LIVING accommodations consisted of a two-room suite, a sitting room and a bedroom with a private bath. Maribeth was surprised to see the six people and two cats at her door and was even more surprised when Chief Martin told her they were there to take a look at Perry's room.

"We'll only be a short while," the chief assured Maribeth. "We only want to have a quick look around."

When they entered the living room of Perry's suite, Chief Martin flipped the wall switch and light flooded the space. A small sofa and a chair took up the left side of the room and a long computer desk stood along the opposite wall. Framed photographs hung on the wall over the desk. The doorway led into the bedroom where a double bed sat in the middle of the room with a small side table next to it. A six-drawer dresser stood against the right side wall and a closet was positioned on the left side next to the door leading to the small bathroom.

"It's quite a nice setup," Ellie said glancing around.

With her heart racing, Angie stood quietly at the entrance to the bedroom staring at the bed where they'd found Perry. Circe and Euclid stepped into the room, sniffing here and there around the rug and the furniture.

"Do you want to go in?" Chief Martin came up beside Angie. "I'll go in with you."

Angie nodded and they walked slowly over to the bed. The image of Perry lying there cold and still flashed through Angie's mind and sent a shudder through her muscles. Trying to slow her breathing, she closed her eyes to block everything out.

What went on in here?

Quick visions popped in her brain like fireworks going off. Perry at his desk. Someone at the doorway. A question. Resentment. Perry resting on his bed with the back of his hand over his forehead. A shadow entering the room. An odor.

Angie's eyes flicked open and a short gasp escaped from her throat.

"Are you okay?" the chief asked.

"Do you smell something?"

The chief took a couple of seconds to answer. "Only a bit of a musty smell like the room's been closed up. Is that what you mean?"

"No. I smell something else. Hair spray? Paint thinner? Something medicinal?" Angie ran her hand through her hair while trying to determine what the odor was.

"I don't smell anything either, sis," Courtney said as she and Ellie moved to the entrance to the room.

"Where's Jenna?" Angie asked.

"I'm here. Do you need me?" Jenna walked past her two sisters and before Angie could say anything, the brunette scrunched up her nose. "What's that smell?"

A look of relief washed over Angie and she let out a sigh. "What does it smell like to you?"

Jenna sniffed. "Nail polish remover? Medicine? Where is it coming from?"

"From the night Perry died," Angie said.

"Oh." Jenna moved closer to her twin.

A scratching noise caused Angie, Jenna, and the chief to look across the room to where Circe pawed furiously under the radiator near the window.

Euclid released a shrieking howl and Jenna reached for her sister's hand. "What's wrong with them?"

When Chief Martin hurried over to the animals, Circe stopped her pawing and looked up at the man. The chief knelt and looked under the heater, then he pulled a handkerchief from his back pocket and poked at something until it slipped out from beneath the radiator.

He stood and held the object out for the others to see.

"What is it?" Jenna asked.

"Thanks, you two." Chief Martin smiled down at the cats before answering Jenna's question. "It looks to be the plastic top to a syringe ... most likely the syringe used to inject Perry with. And hopefully, it has someone's fingerprints on it."

10

It was late afternoon when Angie joined Jenna in her jewelry studio in the room at the back of the Victorian. The studio had big windows that offered a pretty view of the flower gardens Ellie had planted and there was a fireplace on the far wall with a round wooden table in front of it where the sisters often sat and helped Jenna with the jewelry production.

Jenna sat at a desk near the window sketching new designs on her pad, and next to her on the windowsill were glass jars and bottles filled with colorful sea glass the sisters had gathered with their nana over the years. More than once, the sea glass had sparkled and shimmered and shafts of light from the multicolored pieces shot about the room.

When the strange display would finish, the ghost of their nana would be in the room with them. It hadn't happened since last Christmas, but they knew Nana would return one day.

Angie sat at the desk opposite Jenna's putting together necklaces and bracelets following her sister's designs. She glanced over to the sofa by the window where the two cats were snoozing. "I'd love to be able to take a nap any time I wanted to."

Jenna took a quick look at Circe and Euclid stretched out over the couch. "No doubt about it, they have the life."

Angie brought up what had been on her mind since visiting Perry's suite of rooms in the boarding house. "Why can't the others smell that odor in Perry's bedroom?"

Jenna stopped drawing and fiddled with her pencil. "It must be a paranormal skill we're developing. We're twins. Maybe some of our skills will overlap."

"Why do we smell it?" Angie asked. "What does it represent?"

Jenna absentmindedly tapped the eraser end of the pencil on her pad. "It's sort of a medicinal smell. Could we be picking up on the substance that was injected into Perry? Is that what we're smelling?"

"It might be." Angie gave a nod. "Could it be something else though? Could it be related somehow to the person who killed Perry?"

"Are we sure he was killed?" Jenna tilted her head in question thinking about the possibility. "Could he have injected himself with too much medicine accidentally?"

"If he did, where's the syringe?"

"Like we've said before, someone might have come by Perry's room and removed it for any number of reasons," Jenna said. "There's also the suicide note on the laptop, but Courtney is adamant that someone other than Perry wrote it." Letting out a sigh, she said, "I guess he *was* killed." Jenna pushed her long brown braid over her shoulder. "You think the odor was left behind by the killer?"

"I wonder. What would make the smell attach to the person?" Angie asked.

"What if he or she is a hairstylist?" Jenna asked. "The smells of shampoo and conditioners and hair-spray might permeate the person's clothes and hair and then traces of the smells get left behind in rooms the person was in?"

"That's a good idea," Angie said. "The killer might work in an art gallery or an art studio. The odor of paints, thinners, glue ... they could all attach to the person while he or she is working." Making eye contact with her sister, she said, "What about hospital smells like medicine, sanitizers, things like that? The person could work in a hospital or be an EMT or work as a dentist."

"Yeah. All those things. It's not exactly narrowing down a suspect, is it?" Jenna asked.

"Megan Milton is a pharmacy student," Angie said with a pointed expression. "She has access to medication and she admits to wishing there was more to her relationship with Perry than only being friends."

"But her admission shows us she's not trying to hide anything," Jenna pointed out as she watched her sister place the glass beads on the wire. "Do you think those colors go together? Is it too bold?"

"It's perfect," Angie said reaching across the mat for a tool. "Don't second-guess yourself."

Jenna returned to her sketching. "If I had something to do with Perry's death, I wouldn't spill my guts about how I wished he and I could've dated. It could make the police suspicious of me. If Megan had a hand in killing Perry, I think she would be more careful about relating her desires."

"She does seem pretty open when she talks to us," Angie twisted the end of the wire on the bracelet. "But sometimes, I feel like she's holding back. Maybe she's not telling us everything."

"Did you tell Chief Martin your concerns about her?" Jenna asked. "He might want to chat with her again."

The conversation moved to Angie's bake shop and the satellite shop opening in the museum.

"The people at the museum seem very friendly and helpful and it seems like a great opportunity." Angie laid out the beads and silver findings on the mat for the next bracelet.

"I hear a *but* in there," Jenna noted.

"But is this the right time to expand?"

"Why wouldn't it be? Seize the opportunity when it's placed in your lap."

Angie looked at her sister. "What if Josh and I have a child soon?"

Jenna lifted her eyes to her twin as a smile spread across her face. "Are you...?"

"No, I'm not pregnant, but we'd like to start a family soon. Will I be biting off more than I can handle if we have a baby and I have two shops to run?"

"You have Louisa. She's a great worker. You can depend on her. The two of you can run the businesses."

"What if Louisa marries Lance and she has a child?" Angie worried.

Jenna chuckled. "You can't plan for every contingency. You have to live your life. Louisa probably *will* marry Lance and they probably *will* have a baby. You'll hire more help. And we're all around. Mr. Finch talks about cutting back his hours at the candy store and passing more responsibility to Courtney. That was his plan from the beginning. He'd love to help with a child and with the bake shop."

A light breeze moved the branches of a tree in the yard causing the sunlight to come through the window and hit the sea glass jars at a different angle and, for a moment, Jenna and Angie thought Nana was about to make an appearance.

"It's just the outside light," Angie said with disappointment.

"I wondered if we were about to have a visitor." Jenna kept her eyes on the sea glass just in case. "But I guess not."

Angie's face looked a little sad. "For a second, I thought our talk of babies might be drawing Nana to us." Last winter, Angie, in grave danger from an unknown foe, received help from two unexpected sources ... the ghost of her nana and the spirit of her future daughter.

Courtney entered the jewelry studio carrying a silver tray holding several different kinds of sweets, some cups and saucers, and a sugar and creamer. "What's cookin' in here?"

"We're working." Jenna grinned at the tray in her sister's hands. "But it might be time for a break. What have you got there?"

Mr. Finch followed Courtney into the room holding his cane in one hand and a coffee pot in the other. "We have some new candy for you to taste test. We've left some in the dining room for the B and B guests to give their opinions as well, but of course, we value what you think the most, so here we are."

Putting the tray on the desk, Courtney looked at Angie and asked, "What's wrong with you?"

"Nothing." Angie was surprised by the question. "Why?"

"Your face looks sad." Courtney put the back of her hand on Angie's cheeks and then checked her forehead. "You don't have a temperature."

"I'm fine." Angie playfully batted away her sister's hand. "We were talking about Nana."

"Why?"

"No reason. We were just chatting." Angie moved the cups from the tray to the top of the desk.

Finch poured coffee into the cups. "It has been a while since your nana has paid us a visit. Although she didn't show herself, I believe she was present at your wedding," he told Angie.

"I agree, Mr. Finch." Angie's face brightened. "I could feel her near me ... and our mom, too."

The cats trilled from the sofa.

Courtney moved the plate of sweets to the desk and explained what she and Mr. Finch had created. "And this one has several layers of fudge alternating with thin layers of vanilla cake. Then we covered it with chocolate ganache. It's a modern twist on petit-fours."

Jenna's eyes widened. "I'll try that one first."

The foursome sipped coffee and nibbled on the sweets, and Angie and Jenna gave their opinions on the new creations ... which were all favorable and full of praise for the candy makers.

"You two like everything." Courtney shook her head. "You're no help at all. I don't know why we even ask you."

"If something wasn't good, we'd tell you," Jenna mumbled as she chewed one of the caramel candies.

"I don't think your taste is discriminating enough

for our products," Courtney teased causing Mr. Finch to chuckle.

Euclid and Circe stood up on the sofa and stared towards the threshold of the doorway, and two seconds later, Ellie walked into the room holding a phone. "You left your phone in the kitchen," she told Angie. "There's a text from Chief Martin. He wants you to come to the police station. Maura Norris, Perry's former girlfriend, just showed up there."

Adrenaline hurried through Angie's veins as everyone shared worried looks with one another, and then she stood up to go to the police station.

11

_____

When Jenna and Angie arrived at the station, a woman in her late-twenties with short, white blond hair that made her look like a pixie sat on the vinyl seat in the waiting room checking her phone. Angie looked to the desk clerk who nodded his head at the woman indicating that she was Maura Norris.

"Maura?" Angie stepped over to introduce herself and her sister.

The slim, average-height woman looked up and stood. With a pleasant smile, she said, "I'm Maura. Chief Martin and I just finished talking and he told me you'd be along. He had another meeting so I waited out here."

"There's a small conference room we could use,

but it's so nice outside, would you like to take a walk with us. We can chat while we walk," Angie said.

Maura's face lit up at the suggestion. "I'd love that. I'm always cooped up inside. Walking around would be great."

Jenna suggested a stroll to Coveside, a pretty area of Sweet Cove down by the harbor with shops and stores, brick sidewalks, and gardens.

"I haven't been to Coveside in almost a year." Maura checked the store windows as they walked past. "I'm in Boston now doing my residency. I don't have time for a getaway or a weekend trip."

"We're sorry about Perry," Angie told the woman. "We understand you and he had dated."

"We did." Maura ran her hand over the side of her hair. "We were together for a little over a year and a half. We were both working so hard all the time that we didn't really have the time or energy to foster a relationship. Perry and I had an attraction to one another and even though I knew it would never last, I was drawn into seeing him. He was a great guy." Maura shook her head and touched a finger to her eyes. "Who would ever imagine this would happen to him."

"Did Chief Martin ask you to come up?" Jenna

asked trying to clarify how Maura's and the chief's meeting came about.

"I came up on a whim. Several meetings I had got cancelled so I decided to drive up to speak with the chief," Maura said. "He's a very nice man. At least, he seems so. Do you have a different opinion of him?"

"Our opinion matches yours," Angie said with a smile. "Chief Martin is one of the very good guys."

"I'm usually a decent judge of character, but sometimes people can pull the wool over your eyes." Maura looked at the boats bobbing in the harbor. "Such a pretty place."

"What did you want to say to Chief Martin?" Angie questioned.

Maura turned her dark brown eyes to Angie. "I wanted to know what happened to Perry. I wanted to know what the investigation had discovered."

"Did he tell you?" Jenna asked.

"I'm not next-of-kin and I was no longer dating Perry so the chief wasn't inclined to share much with me," Maura said, "but he was kind enough to tell me some things. The boarding house owner, Maribeth, asked you for help the morning she found Perry unconscious?"

"She did," Angie said. "I was with a family friend.

When we arrived at the boarding house, Maribeth was distraught. She asked us to see Perry."

Maura stopped walking and faced the sisters, and they moved to the side so as not to block the walkway. "How did he look? Was he breathing? Was he alive when you saw him?"

"I'm not medically trained," Angie said. "Perry felt cold. He was pale. I tried to find a pulse, but...." She gave a shrug. "I began chest compressions and my friend called the emergency number for an ambulance."

Maura's chest visibly rose and fell as her lips quivered slightly. "Did Perry respond in anyway?"

Angie shook her head.

"Megan Milton was there?" Maura asked. "She helped?"

"We took turns doing the compressions," Angie told her. "You know Megan?"

"I had a small apartment in Silver Cove when I was in med school, but I spent a good amount of time at the boarding house with Perry. I studied there, ate there, stayed over sometimes. Perry and I took turns staying at each other's places. I was familiar with Maribeth and the boarders," Maura said.

"Are you and Megan friendly?" Jenna asked.

Maura sighed and rolled her eyes. "As friendly as you can be with someone who is after your boyfriend."

Angie indicated a small park with a few benches facing the water and they went to sit. "Megan was interested in Perry?"

"She pretended they were just pals." Maura narrowed her brown eyes. "But she couldn't hide that she was very attracted to Perry."

"Did you talk to Perry about her?" Jenna questioned.

"I brought it up, yeah. Perry would blow it off. I honestly didn't feel comfortable with Megan living in the room across from Perry. I trusted him, but she was always bouncing in, stopping by, asking him to make dinner with her, asking him to study with her."

"Did you ever talk to Megan about her behavior?"

"There was no point. If I did, she would have gotten defensive and Perry would have been annoyed that I confronted her. There was no winning so I kept quiet," Maura said. "Anyway, people are going to do what they're going to do. You can't force someone to stay with you. You have to take the good with the bad and hope for the best.

And like I said, from the beginning, I didn't think Perry and I had a future together."

The young women watched a sailboat head out of the harbor moving gracefully past the other boats.

"Why did you think there was no future?" Jenna asked Maura.

"Perry was single-minded, focused like a laser on his studies, on his work. The work was number one. I wasn't even number two. I was a very distant number three."

"What was number two?" Angie asked.

"You know Perry had headaches?" When Angie and Jenna nodded, Maura went on. "They were severe. He had them fairly often. Taking care of himself was his second obsession. He was very attentive to his health, he was very careful about what he ate, he made sure he exercised each day and got enough sleep. If he missed too much at school, he would have fallen too far behind and he *wasn't* going to do that. Perry was determined. He was going to be a doctor." Maura shrugged. "School and his health. Everything else came after those two things and a lot of the time, he had no energy to give to anything but school and taking care of himself. I knew all of this when I started dating him."

"Why did you bother dating Perry?" Angie asked.

"There must have been other med students who were open to developing a relationship."

Maura stretched her legs out in front of her. "I think because I'm a lot like Perry. I'm determined as well. The schooling, the residency, all the training ... becoming a doctor is not for the faint of heart. It's grueling, relentless work. I dated Perry as an outlet, to relax, to have a little fun. I knew he wouldn't demand anything of me. He was safe." Maura looked pointedly at the two sisters. "But that didn't mean I was okay with someone like Megan trying to push me aside and move in on Perry."

"Why did you break up?"

"I was moving to Boston for the residency," Maura said. "It would never work out with me in Boston and Perry up here. We both knew that."

"Was it an amicable parting of the ways?" Jenna asked.

"It was. Even though I knew that's how it would end, it was still sad." Maura's face looked thoughtful.

"Your field is anesthesiology?" Jenna asked.

"That's the goal." Maura's mouth turned up a little. "If I make it."

"You mentioned knowing the other residents in the boarding house," Angie said. "How did you get on with them? Did you get to know them?"

"Somewhat. Everyone would get together for dinner at least once a week. Sometimes the group would watch a movie together, or do a puzzle, play cards."

"What did you think of them?"

"Roger and Mary, they're the older people in the house, they got on each other's nerves a lot," Maura said with a smile. "I could never figure out if they just enjoyed fussing at each other or if they had an actual dislike for one another."

"Did they get along with Perry?" Angie asked.

"Mary did. Roger had a persnickety personality that sometimes Perry tired of. But Perry never let on he was annoyed with the man."

"Do you know Andy Hobbs?" Jenna asked.

"I know him, sure. He lived in the boarding house."

"What do you think of him?"

Maura raised an eyebrow. "Andy is full of himself, loves himself actually. We could joke around, but he isn't someone I'd want as a friend. Too selfish, too arrogant."

Angie nodded and asked, "Did Megan take part in the games or watching the movie with the group?"

Maura gave a sly smile. "If Perry was there, then she'd be there, too."

"How about Maribeth?" Angie asked. "Did she join in?"

"Oh, sure."

"And did she get along well with Perry?" Jenna asked.

Maura hesitated for a few moments. "She did, but sometimes Maribeth picked at Perry, giving him digs once in a while about not helping out enough at the boarding house."

Angie looked confused. "Why would she expect Perry to help out?"

"Perry got a slight discount on the rent because when he moved in, he agreed to do some things around the house to get a break on the cost of living there," Maura said. "Maribeth didn't think he was doing enough to get the discount so she raised his rent. Perry was annoyed about that, and Maribeth was annoyed that he was annoyed. I guess it's not unusual for people to bicker when they live in close quarters."

"Did Chief Martin ask you if you suspect someone in Perry's death?" Jenna asked.

Maura took in a quick breath. "He *did* ask."

"What was your answer?" Angie asked.

Looking down at her hands, Maura didn't answer right away. "I told the chief I wasn't sure of anything, but Megan keeps popping into my mind. She fell for Perry and he didn't reciprocate her affection. Did she lose it that night? Did she get so angry that she decided to...."

"Did Perry self-medicate for his headaches?" Angie asked. "Did he have the drugs in his room? Did he inject himself sometimes when he got a bad headache?"

Maura swallowed hard and flicked her eyes over the garden flowers. "If Perry did that, it wouldn't be out of the realm of possibility that he would have been kicked out of school for injecting himself with medication. Perry was a medical *student*, he was not yet a doctor."

Angie watched Maura's face. "So you don't know if he did or not?"

"I told him never to do it when I was around or I'd have to report him," Maura said. "I turned a blind eye to what he might have needed to do to function."

"Did you ever help Perry with the drugs?" Angie asked.

Maura's eyes flashed. "No. I wasn't going to get into trouble over it. I wasn't going to jeopardize my future should the school think I was complicit if Perry self-medicated."

Jenna shifted slightly on the bench to face

Maura. "Then Perry *did* use injections to treat himself."

Maura crossed her arms over her chest. "I'm not going to say anything about that one way or the other."

And by Maura not replying to the question, Angie and Jenna knew the answer.

12

_____

The sun had only been up for a short time when Angie placed the boxes of muffins, rolls, scones, and a coffee cake on the boarding house's kitchen counter while Maribeth took out some platters from the cabinet.

"Ellie sent over an egg, cheese, and onion quiche and a pot of beef stew," Angie gestured to the items she'd brought in from the car on her first trip inside.

"Oh, gosh. Please tell her thank you from me," Maribeth said. "You've all been so nice. I appreciate it. I just don't feel like cooking anymore."

"Your energy will come back when it's ready," Angie smiled at the woman. "Wait and see."

"I'm tired all the time." Maribeth removed the muffins and rolls and set them in a basket.

"It will pass eventually." Angie gave Maribeth a kind pat on the shoulder.

"I feel so guilty that someone died in my house." Maribeth's voice hitched.

"It's not your fault," Angie said. "You did everything you could possibly do to keep the boarders safe."

Maribeth nodded her head, but Angie knew her words hadn't comforted the woman ... only the passing of time would manage to lessen her sadness and guilt.

"I'm going to the basement to toss in some laundry and do some ironing," Maribeth said. "There's fresh brewed coffee in the pot. Help yourself. Stay as long as you like, and thanks again for your kindness."

Chief Martin had asked Angie to talk to any of the boarders she ran into when delivering pastries and sweets to the boarding house so she poured some coffee and sat at the kitchen island hoping someone would come for breakfast. In less than ten minutes, Andy Hobbs walked in wearing sweatpants with his hair askew and his eyes looking sleepy. He stopped short and stared at Angie for a few seconds.

"Oh, it's you."

Angie smiled and said, "Good morning. I made a

delivery. Maribeth put everything out on the counter."

"Excellent." Andy grabbed a plate and filled it. "I love your stuff." He poured coffee and took a stool at the island next to Angie.

After a few minutes of conversation, Andy said, "The police haven't figured out what happened to Perry yet."

"It was an overdose of medication," Angie told him.

"I heard that at school." The nursing school Andy attended was in the same building as the medical school Perry studied at. "Everyone's talking about it. But what actually happened? Did he give himself the overdose or did someone give it to him? And if he did give himself the meds, did he give too much accidentally or on purpose? I heard there's a suicide note."

Angie didn't want to confirm or deny the existence of the note. "I heard that as well."

"What do you think happened? You think Perry killed himself?"

"I didn't know him," Angie said. "But from what I've heard about his drive and ambition, I wouldn't think he wanted to end his life."

Andy shrugged as he buttered his scones.

"Maybe Perry didn't think he had what it takes to be a doctor and he fell into despair."

"You think so?" Angie swiveled the stool a little to face Andy. "Did you think Perry was acting differently than usual?"

"I don't know the inner workings of someone's brain." Andy bit into the scone.

"Do you think Perry was depressed?"

"Hard to tell. The guy was always working. Well, not always, but he often seemed distracted, like he was thinking about his work all the time."

"Did you interact with him much?" Angie asked.

"Not a ton. He was in his room a lot. He always struck me as kind of arrogant," Andy said with a frown. "I got the impression he thought he was better than everyone because he was in med school."

"What gave you that feeling?"

"I tried to strike up conversations with him, but he seemed reluctant to engage with me. I don't know. Just my impression. Maybe it had nothing to do with what we were each studying. Maybe it was a personality conflict."

"Did you argue?"

"Nothing like that. Perry wasn't that friendly, at least not to me." Andy dipped a piece of his scone in his coffee mug. "I did like his old girlfriend though.

She was funny. We could joke around together. She had a good sense of humor."

"Do you think Perry might have been jealous of you? Of your easy friendship with his girlfriend?" Angie questioned.

"Never thought of it that way." Andy smiled. "I hope he was jealous. Maura was too good for him. He didn't give her enough attention."

Angie cocked her head to the side. "Maybe Maura didn't want any more than what she got from Perry."

"That wasn't it. Maura told me she wished Perry would be more serious about the relationship. She wanted a commitment ... or at least, the idea of a commitment down the line."

"I met Maura recently," Angie said. "She told me she *didn't* want a serious relationship. It wasn't the time for something like that. She had to focus on her residency."

Andy made eye contact with the young woman sitting next to him. "Maura's telling you a tale."

"Maybe she told *you* a tale," Angie countered.

Andy let out a chuckle. "Maura and I were friendly. I knew her for a while before she moved to Boston for her residency. I think she'd be more upfront with me than with you."

"Could be." Angie sipped her coffee. "Was there anyone you can think of who might want Perry dead?"

"Me," Andy smirked and when Angie gave him a look, he said, "Kidding. I wouldn't have minded dating Maura, but she was out of the picture by the time Perry died. I hadn't seen her for a while."

"You could call her," Angie suggested.

"Whatever. That ship has sailed." Andy got up to fill his cup.

"Can you think of anyone besides yourself who might want Perry dead?" Angie asked.

"A lot of people thought Perry was a nice guy, but there were some who thought differently. The guy wasn't much of a team player. He wasn't helpful to his cohort. Everything was a competition with him and he was going to be the best. He clashed with one student in particular. That's the rumor anyway."

Angie's ears perked up. "Who was the student?"

"Another guy. Charles something or other."

"How did they clash?"

"I don't have details. Anyway, who knows. The police will figure it out one of these days, if they ever get off their duffs." Andy took another muffin and headed to the hallway. "I gotta get going."

Angie was not sorry to see Andy leave for his

classes. He struck her as insensitive and a little arrogant, and almost like he had a chip on his shoulder. A housemate had just passed away, but it didn't seem to bother Andy Hobbs one bit. Angie wondered what sort of nurse he would make if he couldn't show a little empathy for someone's misfortune.

~

WHEN ANGIE CLOSED the bake shop for the day and went into the Victorian's adjoining kitchen, she greeted the cats who arched their backs into big stretches.

"They were snoozing on the fridge," Courtney said from her seat at the kitchen table. "I'm surprised they got up to say hello to you."

"That's because I'm their favorite," Angie patted the felines' heads.

"Sorry to break it to you, sis, but I think Mr. Finch is their favorite," Courtney joked. "But if it makes you happy, you can pretend they like you best."

"They can have two favorites," Angie smiled and removed her apron.

"Did you talk to anyone at the boarding house

this morning?" Courtney asked. "Were you able to corral anyone there?"

Angie told her sister about her conversation with Andy Hobbs and then told her that she didn't like the man. "He's very insensitive."

"I got the same impression of him when I met him the other day." Courtney said, "So what are you thinking about all of this? We found a cap to a syringe in Perry's room, well, Circe found it. And Maura implied to you that Perry was self-medicating. If that's the case, the drugs and the syringes must have been in Perry's room and his friends must have known they were there. It would be easy for someone to sneak in and inject him with an overdose while Perry was sleeping."

"What's the motivation though?" Angie asked. "That's the key. Once we can answer that, then we'll probably know who the killer is."

"He didn't kill himself," Courtney said. "If we focus on that, we'll go down the wrong path." She reached into a folder she had on the table next to her and took out a piece of paper. "This a printout of the note that was on Perry's laptop. I've been reading it over and over."

Angie looked at the paper with interest. "And?"

"And from what people have said about Perry, I don't think he wrote this."

"Why not?"

"The way the sentences are formulated, the words used in the note. Remember when I was taking that anthropology course in college? Communication was discussed. Most people have different ways of stringing words together to make sentences. Take you and Ellie for example. Ellie has a more formal way of talking. If she wrote a note on a certain subject and you wrote a note on the same subject, we'd all be able to pick out which one of you wrote which note."

"I get it." Angie nodded. "I see what you mean. But you didn't know Perry. You can't be that sure he didn't write this." She gestured to the paper.

Courtney folded her arms and leaned onto the table. "I have a *feeling*. I know I'm right."

Angie raised an eyebrow in thought and then she said, "What if you could get a few samples of Perry's writing, some emails he sent to friends and to professors, maybe a sample of a paper he wrote for a class. Take a look at them, get a feel for the way he communicated and compare it to this note."

"I could ask Chief Martin if he could show me

some examples of Perry's writing from his laptop," Courtney's eyes were bright. "It's a great idea."

"If the writing samples are different from the suicide note, then we'll know someone who had access to Perry's laptop wrote the fake note," Angie said.

Courtney's tone was full of excitement. "And that same person must have killed Perry."

The cats meowed their approval from their positions back on top of the refrigerator.

13

In the waning early evening light, Mr. Finch, Angie, Courtney, and Jenna sat in Finch's sunroom painting and drawing at the long table and at easels, and Ellie perched at the edge of her chair with her cello in front of her practicing new music. Near the big open windows, the two cats rested on the back of the sofa keeping their eyes on the birds and squirrels moving about the backyard. Betty, Finch's girlfriend and a successful real estate agent and broker, was at the dining room table doing paperwork, returning emails, and making calls to clients.

Finch worked at an easel on a large seascape while Angie used a charcoal pencil to draw a picture of Euclid and Circe sitting under the pergola behind the Victorian. Courtney practiced her new interest in calligraphy and Jenna used colored pencils to sketch out some new jewelry designs for the fall line.

"This is a most pleasant way to spend a few hours," Finch said as he sat back to check his painting. "Your cello playing is just lovely," he told Ellie.

"I've been trying to master this piece and I think I'm almost there." With a satisfied smile, Ellie rested the cello to the side and placed her bow against the chair next to her.

"Shall we take a break and have refreshments?" Finch asked.

Finch and Courtney brought in crackers and cheese, fruit, lemonade and iced tea and everyone settled at the round table. Although there had been no discussion of crime or murder all afternoon with the group wanting a break from such talk, they all knew it was time to bring up the subject of Perry Wildwood.

Courtney went through the reasons she suspected the suicide note was a fake which had been written by someone else to throw off the authorities. "The way people describe Perry makes me think the note is worded in a way that isn't consistent with the way Perry would write it."

"That's a very interesting viewpoint." Finch

poured lemonade into his glass. "And I think you're on to something."

Courtney gave a nod. "I'm meeting with the chief tomorrow to take a look at other things Perry wrote on his laptop. That way I can compare the language he used to the suicide note. I'd bet money that the word use and arrangement in the other written pieces will be different from the note."

"I think this idea has a lot of merit," Jenna praised her sister. "It's very clever."

"From the beginning, I didn't think the note was written by Perry," Courtney said. "I had a hunch about it, I guess. Now we just have to prove it."

"What about motivations?" Ellie asked. "Who could have had motivation to kill Perry?"

"We have nothing concrete," Angie said, "only suspicions."

"Megan Milton claims she had an interest in Perry, but respected that he didn't want a relationship so remained within the bounds of friendship only," Jenna said.

Courtney added, "But Perry's former girlfriend, Maura Norris, told us Megan was clearly after Perry, and that she acted in such a bold way that it made Maura uncomfortable."

"What about Maura?" Ellie asked. "Was she

upset with Perry for only wanting a casual relationship?"

Angie's face wore a serious expression while she thought about her interaction with Maura. "She claims to have wanted the same thing as Perry, nothing serious, a fun, easy-going relationship with no strings attached and no plans for the future." Tilting her head to the side, Angie added, "But I'm not sure I believe that's really what she wanted."

"I got the same feeling," Courtney said. "I wouldn't be one bit surprised if Maura was the one who injected Perry with an overdose. Maybe she's good at hiding her real feelings."

"Who else do you suspect?" Finch asked.

"I don't like Andy Hobbs." Angie's lips were tight and her eyes darkened. "I don't trust him. He didn't like Perry and he was flip about Perry's death. It's like it doesn't faze him at all. He doesn't seem to feel an ounce of sympathy or empathy over the death. He doesn't care that a housemate died, or that he might have been killed."

"Why does a guy like that choose to go into the nursing profession where he'll have to care for people?" Ellie asked. "It doesn't seem to fit with his personality."

"For the money, I bet. He'll have a stable, solid

salary." Courtney moved to the sofa to pat the cats. "Maybe he plans to go into administration where he won't be involved with actual patient care."

"I hope that's it," Angie said with a shake of her head. "Andy would not have a very kind or caring bedside manner."

"What about the other boarding house residents?" Finch asked. "Would they have had access to Perry's laptop? Could one of them have written the note?"

"We haven't talked to the other two residents yet," Angie said, "but Maribeth told us that the residents left their laptops or books or other personal things laying around the house. Perry never locked the door to his room. No one expected any of the other boarders to steal anything, so yes, I think the older residents could have accessed Perry's laptop."

"When Mr. Finch touched the laptop, he sensed someone who was angry and jealous of Perry had used it," Courtney said. "It could have been someone in the boarding house. One of them could have written that suicide note."

"When does Chief Martin want you to speak with the older boarders?" Finch asked.

Angie said, "We've set up separate appointments

for tomorrow and the day after with Roger Winthrop and Mary Bishop."

"Mrs. Bishop and Mr. Winthrop seemed slightly irritated with one another when Miss Angie and I were at the house the morning after the killing," Finch said.

Courtney chuckled. "Shouldn't you be calling Angie *Mrs. Angie* now that she's married, Mr. Finch?"

Finch's mustache moved slightly when he smiled. "It doesn't sound right to my ear. I still refer to Jenna as *Miss Jenna* even though she is married as well."

"How about *Ms.* Angie and *Ms.* Jenna?" Courtney asked. "It has a good ring to it."

"That might be a possibility," Finch nodded. "I will consider it."

Angie ignored Courtney's suggestions to Mr. Finch. "I picked up the same thought about Mary's and Roger's relationship. They seemed impatient and annoyed with one another."

"Since they're not friends, maybe one of them will spill some information about the other," Jenna said.

"A couple of people have implied that Perry and Maribeth weren't on the best of terms," Angie revealed. "Perry got a break on the rent because he was supposed to help out around the house, but it seems he didn't do what he was supposed to do and Maribeth wasn't happy with him."

"I can't believe that would be reason to kill the man," Ellie said.

"They might have been arguing and then things escalated," Courtney pointed out. "Maribeth mentioned she had been a nurse. She would recognize the medications Perry had in his room and she would know how to use a syringe."

Angie's face paled slightly considering Maribeth as a killer. "I can't wrap my head around that. It can't be Maribeth."

"Don't dismiss anyone until we're sure," Courtney warned. "Some people are very good at hiding who they are and what they're capable of."

With a sad frown and a sigh, Finch said, "I understand that all too well."

"I didn't mean to make you sad, Mr. Finch." Courtney got up from the sofa and gave the man a hug.

Finch's brother, Thaddeus, was a mean and terrible man who attempted to kill Finch by pushing him down a long and steep flight of stairs when they were young men. The injuries resulted in a permanent limp and necessitated the use of a cane for the rest of Finch's adult life. Thaddeus's evil ways caught up with him in Sweet Cove when someone murdered him in the candy store with a knife. The good Finch inherited the store and invited Courtney to become his co-owner.

"I am continually baffled by how different two people born to the same parents can be," Finch said softly. "My brother was a monster. A terrible person who cared nothing for the people around him."

"I'm so sorry you had someone like that in your life." Courtney gently rubbed the older man's shoulder.

"Yes." Finch looked lost in thought as he patted the young woman's hand, but then he took in a deep breath and said, "But the events of my life brought me here to all of you. One must take the bitter with the sweet."

Courtney said, "Maribeth said that to us, too. I'd never heard the saying before."

"No life is perfect," Finch said as Circe came over to jump onto his lap. "It is a mix of good things and bad, of sadness and joy." Looking around the sunroom at each of the Roseland sisters, a smile lifted the man's lips and a twinkle returned to his eyes. "I prefer to focus on the joy. Being part of your family has been the blessing of my life, a blessing I never expected."

"We wouldn't have it any other way," Angie smiled warmly at Finch. "I don't know what we'd do without you, Mr. Finch."

Circe stood on the man's lap, put her little paws on his chest, and sweetly rubbed her cheek against his chin.

14

Angie and Mr. Finch sat in the boarding house's den with seventy-four-year old Mary Bishop, a slim, short, light-haired blonde with soft brown eyes who was dressed in black slacks and a perfectly-pressed pale blue, long-sleeved shirt. She wrung her hands together as they rested in her lap.

"I haven't felt comfortable in the house since Perry's passing. I'm having a hard time sleeping. I wake up in the middle of the night feeling either terrified or full of anxiety," Mary said. "I moved here nearly two years ago shortly after my husband died. I didn't want to live alone. Having people around is important to me. It makes me feel better to interact with others, but now I worry that I'm not safe here. Is there a murderer living under this roof?"

Angie used a gentle tone when she asked, "When you think about your housemates, is there someone who gives you cause for concern?"

Mary's eyes widened. "I don't know. Maybe?"

"Who in the house makes you feel worried?" Finch asked.

"I don't know," Mary nearly wailed.

"Do you think maybe your concern doesn't come from the housemates, but from not knowing what happened to Perry?" Angie tried to get at the root of the older woman's nervousness. "Is it the uncertainty surrounding Perry's death that's causing your worry?"

"Maybe." Mary's eyes flicked around the room. "But Perry was killed. Why was he? Why would someone do that to him? *Who* did it to him?"

Angie kept her face blank. "The police haven't said Perry was killed."

Mary stared at the young woman and blinked several times. "Well, what else could be the reason for his death?"

"Suicide?" Finch said gently.

"He killed himself?" Mary said breathlessly.

Angie said, "There hasn't been a firm determination on the cause of death yet."

"Perry could have had a fatal reaction to some medication," Finch said. "Or he may have had an accidental overdose. The police are still investigating."

"Maybe no one killed him." Mary seemed to exhale and she moved her hands from her lap to the arms of the cozy chair she was sitting in. "That would be a relief."

"What's it like living here?" Angie asked.

"Oh, you know. It's fine most of the time." It was clear that Mary was dancing around the question.

"And other times?" Finch asked.

"People don't get along with each other one-hundred percent of the time." Mary shrugged a shoulder. "There are squabbles, disappointments, misunderstandings. It happens everywhere humans come together. It's no different here. Sometimes the residents annoy each other, get on one another's nerves. It blows over. It can't be taken too seriously."

"Did some people in the house get into more squabbles than others?" Angie asked.

"Sure. It's human nature. When people gather some irritations arise. It can't be avoided." Mary gave a nod.

"Is there someone who irritates you?" Angie asked.

Mary leaned forward looking appreciative that someone finally asked who irritated *her*. "Andy Hobbs. He can be sullen and unpleasant ... and impatient. How will he ever make it through nursing school? How would he make a good nurse?"

Angie couldn't speak to the comment so she gave a slight shake of her head hoping Mary would go on talking without prompting.

A stubborn look crossed over the older woman's face. "He won't make a good one. Definitely not. If I was a patient in the hospital and Andy was the only nurse left, I'd tell him to go away."

"Have you had a run in with Mr. Hobbs?" Finch questioned.

"Not really." Mary scrunched up her nose. "He has a fresh mouth. He says rude things."

"To you?"

"To everyone," Mary huffed. "Maybe some people think he's funny. He isn't."

"Can you share an example with us?" Angie asked.

"Not off the top of my head." Mary crossed her arms over her chest. "I don't like him. I don't have to like everyone."

"Of course not," Finch agreed.

"Did Andy and Perry get along?" Angie asked.

"They weren't friends. Andy was the same way with Perry. I really don't think they liked each other."

"Did they argue?"

"I never saw them argue," Mary said.

"Did *you* get along with Perry?" Finch asked.

The woman nodded. "Perry was a nice person."

Angie wanted to know how well Mary knew the young medical student. "Did Perry mention his headaches to you?"

"He did. It was hard. I felt sorry for him."

"Do you know if he took any medication specifically for the headaches?"

Mary looked uncomfortable for a second. "I'm not sure. He told me that nothing much helped."

"Did you ever see what he took when he had one of his headaches?" Angie asked.

"Some pills."

"Did he take anything besides pills?"

"I don't know. Sometimes I made him a cup of coffee. Caffeine can help with headaches."

"Your room is on the second floor, is that right?" Angie knew where it was from talking to Chief Martin.

"It is."

"Which side of the house is it on?"

Mary raised her arm and pointed to the west side.

"Right above Perry's room?" Mr. Finch asked.

"Yes. Not exactly above, partially above."

"Did you hear anything the night Perry died?" Angie watched Mary's face.

"The police asked that very same question. I don't recall hearing anything," Mary said.

"Do you usually sleep right through the night?"

"Oh, no. Almost never. I wake up a few times each night. Sometimes I can fall back to sleep and other times I toss and turn for hours." Mary sighed. "What I wouldn't give to fall asleep at night and not wake up until the sun comes up."

"Did you sleep through the night on the evening Perry died?"

"I don't remember. The police asked me that, too."

"So you don't remember anything unusual that night?" Finch asked.

"I don't think so."

"Did everyone else in the house get along with Perry?" Angie asked.

"Pretty much, although Maribeth was annoyed with him a lot of the time."

"Why was she?" Finch questioned.

"Perry got a discount on his rent in exchange for helping around the house and yard," Mary explained. "Only thing was, he didn't do any work. He always said he was too busy. It wasn't fair, really. Maribeth can't do everything and hiring help for yardwork or little things around the house is very expensive. If Perry didn't want to help out, he should have declined the discount. Of course, I never said that to him ... but I thought it."

Angie nodded. "Did you know Perry's girlfriend, Maura Norris?"

"I met her. I didn't think she was right for Perry. She seemed cold. She seemed very ambitious."

"Isn't that a good thing?" Angie asked, keeping an even tone. "To want to better yourself?"

"Yes, of course, but Maura didn't seem like she cared about anyone but herself."

"Do you think Perry loved her?"

"I couldn't answer that. Perry appeared to enjoy her company."

"Do you know who broke off the relationship?" Angie asked.

"I think Perry did. I think he was too busy to have a steady girlfriend," Mary said.

The three people discussed the difficulties of

trying to sustain a relationship while working or studying in a demanding field.

"Did Perry ever date Megan?" Mr. Finch asked. "She seems like a very nice young woman."

Mary leaned forward again and lowered her voice. "You know, Megan had a crush on Perry. Don't tell her I said this. She and I get along great. We share a lot about our lives. I felt bad for her. Megan is a sweetheart. She really fell for Perry, but he didn't return her feelings."

"How did she handle the rejection?" Finch asked.

"I know it hurt her terribly, but Megan is a determined person," Mary said. "I don't think she'd given up on winning Perry over." The woman's eyes turned sad. "Now it's too late for her."

"Did you ever see Perry inject himself with medication?" Angie asked.

Mary eyed Angie. "He wasn't a drug addict."

"Oh, we know that he wasn't," Angie said apologetically. "We think Perry may have used an injectable drug to combat his headaches."

Mary bit her lower lip, quickly shifting her eyes around the room, and then said softly, "Sometimes he did."

Angie wondered why Mary told her earlier that

she didn't know if Perry took other meds besides pills for his head pain. "Did he tell you this?"

"I saw him do it. A couple of times, I filled the syringe for him because he couldn't manage it, his headache was so bad."

"How did you know how to fill a syringe?" Finch asked.

"My dog was diabetic. I had to give him insulin injections twice a day," Mary said.

"What drug was Perry using to help with his pain?" Angie questioned.

Mary scrunched up her forehead in thought. "I don't remember. It was something ... *caine*. Caine was the last part of the word. I don't recall what the first part was." The woman's eyes flashed and she said forcefully, "Perry wasn't a drug addict. Don't go getting the idea he was. He used medication appropriately for his problem, and only when he had a problem."

"Did the injections help?" Finch asked.

Mary said, "A lot of the time, but the degree of help was not consistent. There were times the medication completely took the headache away, and other times, it only made a dent in the pain."

Angie sat straight in her chair. "Did you fill the syringe the night Perry died?"

Mary's face turned to stone. "I did not."

"Why didn't you tell us earlier that Perry used something besides pills to manage his headaches?" Angie asked with a curious tone so as not to seem accusatory.

Mary wrung her hands again in her lap. "I didn't want you to think Perry was a drug abuser. If you thought he abused drugs, then maybe you'd tell Chief Martin and then law enforcement might stop the investigation into his death. I want them to figure this mess out. I want to know what happened to Perry. I want to be able to sleep at night."

When Angie and Finch were about to leave, they shook hands with Mary and thanked her for speaking with them, and once outside, Angie asked the older man a question.

"When you shook hands with Mary, did you sense anything?"

Finch took Angie's arm and held his cane in the other hand. "I have a feeling Mrs. Bishop did not share everything she knows with us."

Exactly.

15

When eighty-two-year old Roger Winthrop stepped onto the side porch of the Victorian and knocked at the door of the bake shop, Angie answered and greeted him.

"Thank you for coming," she told Roger with a smile. "Would you like to sit inside or out here on the porch?"

Roger eyed the table and chairs set up on the porch with the flower boxes on the railing and the pots of colorful blooms. "Outside would be nice. It's not as hot today as it has been. Is the shop closed for the day or do you need to be inside?"

"We closed at 3pm. I'll text Mr. Finch. He's going

to join us." Angie asked Roger to take a seat and told him she'd bring out some refreshments.

Once the three were settled, they talked about her sisters and their businesses, the Victorian mansion and how Angie came to inherit it, and how Mr. Finch had become an honorary member of the family.

"It's all fascinating," Roger said as he sipped his lemonade cooler and took a sugar cookie from the plate in the center of the table. "You're very lucky, Mr. Finch."

"Please call me Victor. And you're quite right. I am a very lucky man."

"That's why I moved into the boarding house," Roger said. "I was tired of living alone and I certainly didn't want to move to California to live with my son. Too far away. Too much change. I didn't want to leave everything I know. I've lived two towns over from Sweet Cove all of my life. This area is my home."

"That's understandable," Finch said.

"Tell me," Roger began, "why did the police ask me to speak with you?"

Angie cleared her throat. "We have experience as consultants to the police doing interviews and research for them. We help out when they need a hand."

"I see." Roger didn't look like he understood any better why Angie and Finch were interviewing him, but he didn't ask any more about it.

Finch asked, "What did you do for work?"

"I had my own business selling medical supplies, did it for over fifty years before I finally retired," Roger said. "My wife died five years ago. I lived alone for two years, then had enough of that and moved into Maribeth's boarding house."

"How do you like it there?" Angie asked.

"I'm glad I did it. I have my privacy when I want it and there are people to talk with when I want that. I like the mixed ages in the house, it's not just a bunch of old people waiting around to die."

Angie smiled inwardly at Roger's bluntness.

"You must have known Perry fairly well since you and he had been at the house the longest," Angie said.

"Megan has lived there almost as long as Perry and there was the other woman who lived there until recently. She left for a nursing home. Agnes had been at the house since Maribeth opened the place to lessees. Someone new has signed a lease for that suite of rooms. It's another older woman in her early seventies."

"Maribeth doesn't lack for renters," Finch noted. "The house has a good reputation."

"Maribeth had some concern that people wouldn't want to live there after what happened to Perry," Angie said.

Roger made a huffing noise. "Folks aren't that sensitive. I could see renters staying away if all of us were being murdered one by one by some nut. That's not the case. A young man passed away. It happens."

"The police are considering that Perry may have been murdered," Angie said.

"It's their job to look into every possibility," Roger said.

"You don't think foul play was involved?" Finch asked.

"I don't think so. Either Perry had a condition that caused him to pass away or perhaps he took too much medication and overdosed."

"I believe the police have determined an overdose was the reason the young man died," Finch said. "Do you think it might have been intentional?"

"You mean did Perry kill himself?" Roger's eyes widened. "If he did overdose, it was an accident. Perry wouldn't take his own life. He just wouldn't."

"What makes you say that?" Angie questioned.

"The guy had plans, goals. He worked hard to reach them. Sure, he had bad headaches. Lots of people have things they have to deal with. Perry wasn't hopeless or tormented or feeling lost. No, he didn't try to end his life. He had too much to live for."

"Do you think he could have hidden his true feelings from everyone?" Angie asked.

"No, I don't. Perry was a serious student, but he had fun. He worked hard, but he was able to enjoy himself, too. He'd watch movies with us, play cards, cook, go out. He had a friend named Charles, another medical student. They did things together on occasion."

"Did you get to know Charles?" Finch asked.

"I didn't. I met him in passing. He visited with Perry in his room sometimes, or they went out."

"What do you think of Andy Hobbs?"

"Andy is on the gruff side. He has a smart mouth. I think that is an attempt to hide an inferiority complex," Roger said.

Angie added the rest of her seltzer from the can to her glass. "You think he doesn't feel good about himself?"

"No, I don't think he does," Roger shook his

head. "Bluster, bullying, antagonizing others ... that behavior often has roots in feelings of low self-esteem."

"Did Andy get along with Perry?" Angie asked.

"He didn't. I think Andy was jealous of Perry because he was going to be a physician. There was no reason for such thinking, but there it was. Andy strikes me as a very intelligent and capable man. If being a doctor was that important to him, he should have applied to medical school."

"Maybe he didn't get in," Finch suggested.

Roger said, "I don't think that's the case. I don't think Andy applied. I think he's the kind of person who won't put himself out there for fear of failure and then takes his disappointment out on other people."

"Did Andy and Perry argue?"

"No, nothing like that. From what I saw, they mostly avoided each other."

"Do you know what medication Perry took for his headaches?" Angie asked.

Roger looked surprised that Angie and Finch would think he knew such a thing. "I don't. Why do you ask?"

"Did anyone in the house help Perry when he had the headaches?"

Roger's eyebrows went up as he thought about the question. "I think Megan Milton would make him tea or get him a glass of water or a cold pack for his head. Mary Bishop would check on him. She'd make him some toast or soup sometimes. My room was upstairs on the second floor so I was either up there or I was in the common areas. I didn't go down the hall to Perry's and Megan's rooms very often. I had no reason to."

"Did you ever see Perry inject himself with medication?" Angie watched for the older man's reaction.

Roger blinked and his face flushed. "You know what? Your question brought a memory forward. I did see Perry with a syringe about a year ago. Huh. I'd forgotten about that. His door was open. When I walked past, I saw Perry sitting in his easy chair. He was holding a syringe and a small vial of something. I kept walking. I thought it had something to do with his medical training."

Angie leaned forward a little. "Was Perry alone in the room?"

"No, he wasn't. Mary Bishop was with him."

"What was she doing?"

"She was sitting opposite Perry. I nodded to them and went to the kitchen."

"Do you and Mary get along?" Angie asked.

"Sure we do. Mary's a nice woman ... smart, a good conversationalist. She knows a good deal about many subjects. Of course, sometimes we disagree on things and well, we both know we won't change the others' mind so we agree to disagree. We are vocal about what we think and things might seem heated when we're discussing certain topics, but we are always respectful of one another." Roger winked. "Some people might think we don't like each other at all. That's not the case."

"Did you know Perry's former girlfriend, Maura Norris?" Finch brought up the woman Perry had a relationship with.

"Yes, I knew her. I didn't care for her. She and Perry were not a good match. Maura wanted a serious relationship. Perry did not."

"Did Perry tell you this?"

"Megan told me."

"Did Megan ever tell you that *she* would like to have a relationship with Perry?"

"She didn't, but I could tell by the way she looked at Perry that she liked him."

Finch adjusted his black-framed eyeglasses. "If the police determined that Perry had been murdered and they asked you to name a suspect, who would you name?"

Roger set his glass down. "Maura. Charles. Megan."

Angie tilted her head. "Why those three?"

"Maura was a woman scorned. Charles seemed odd to me. Megan suffered unrequited love."

"Why was Charles odd?" Finch asked.

"He was moody, sullen, distant, argumentative. He seemed like he could be a loner. I wondered why Perry was friendly with Charles. Maybe he was being kind. I heard Charles arguing with Perry occasionally."

"Do you know what the arguments were about?"

"No idea."

"The three people you named may have had motivation to hurt Perry," Angie said. "But of the three, do you think any of them could really be capable of murder?"

Roger stared at the tabletop and then lifted his eyes to Finch and Angie. "Maura and Charles."

"Why those two?"

Roger shrugged. "Because something important seems to be missing inside of them."

16

"That's what he said," Angie told Chief Martin and Courtney as they headed into the glass and brick building that housed several of the university's academic departments. "He said there's something missing inside of them."

"What does Roger Winthrop mean by that?" Courtney asked. "Like Maura and Charles are missing something that makes them human? Like they're lacking something inside that would stop them from killing someone?"

Angie said, "I asked him to elaborate and that is exactly what he meant. He thinks Charles and Maura might have the capacity to kill someone. It was a shocking statement to hear. I didn't get that impression from Maura when I talked to her a few days ago, but that's how Roger sees her."

"We spoke with Perry's friend, Charles Conte," the chief said. "He seemed a little odd, but highly intelligent and well-spoken. As I told you, Charles claimed he went by Perry's place on the night of the death to pick up a book and then he left and went home."

"What time did he say he was at Perry's?" Courtney asked.

"He didn't remember," the chief said.

Courtney rolled her eyes. "How convenient. Did Charles give a window of time when he might have been there?"

"He wouldn't commit. He said he gets engrossed in his work and doesn't bother to look at the time."

"Right," Courtney said with a disbelieving tone. "If he really is like that, how will he manage to get to the operating room on time when he's a full-fledged doctor? How does he get to his classes or meetings on time if he's so unaware of time? I don't buy it."

"We'll be speaking with him again in two days," the chief said. "Maybe you can sit in on the interview."

"I'd love to." Courtney's face was serious. "When Charles went to get the book, did he notice anything wrong with Perry? Was Perry feeling okay? Did he seem normal?"

Chief Martin held the door open for the young women. "Charles didn't notice anything out of the ordinary."

Courtney shook her head and kidded, "I can see that Charles is our star witness."

Angie changed the subject as they stepped inside the multi-story building.

"How did you find the woman we're going to meet?"

Chief Martin led the way down the hall to the linguistics department. "I called around looking for an expert in this area and was directed to Dr. Elizabeth Lincoln who is a forensic linguist."

"And that means she is able to tell if someone is likely to have written something?" Angie asked.

"It's complicated," Chief Martin said. "I gave her several examples of Perry's writing that we found on his laptop. A paper for a course he took, some emails, the suicide note. She's been studying them and now she's ready to tell us her conclusion."

Arriving at the secretary's desk, the receptionist made a call and escorted them to Dr. Lincoln's office where a tall, thin, woman with shoulder-length, light brown hair wearing black slacks, a light blue blouse, and a blue jacket waited for them at her door. A broad smile crossed her face when she greeted them.

"Please come in." Dr. Lincoln's office was spacious with a large desk covered with papers and books, bookshelves lining three walls, and a sofa and two chairs set in front of the big windows looking out over the campus. "Have a seat."

"I appreciate you taking the time to see us," Chief Martin said.

"I've worked with law enforcement on similar tasks as the one you presented me with," Dr. Lincoln said. "It takes some time to analyze the information and make a determination."

The chief asked, "And you've come to a conclusion about Perry Wildwood's communications?"

"I have." Dr. Lincoln opened her laptop and projected two articles side by side onto the white board against the far wall. "An academic paper would obviously be a more formal piece of writing than would be someone's email correspondence so when doing the analysis, it is important to keep that in mind. Most people write and speak using formal or familiar language depending on the audience. When I give a presentation to my peers, I use more formal syntax and higher level vocabulary than I would if I was speaking with friends when out at a bar for a few drinks."

Angie asked, "Are you able to see enough similarities in language when looking at both formal and informal communication in order to decide that the same person wrote them?"

"Often, yes," Dr. Lincoln said.

"Were you able to do that in Perry's case?" Courtney asked.

"I'll show you." Dr. Lincoln used a laser pointer to focus Angie's, Courtney's, and Chief Martin's attention on certain sections of the correspondence shown on the white board. The woman spoke about word choice and form, sentence construction, word order, syntax. "We're able to see patterns within the formal and informal communication modes that link together and point to whether or not the same person created the written pieces."

"What did you find in Perry's case?" Angie asked.

"Seven of the eight pieces of correspondence have the necessary similarities to be linked together as creations of Perry Wildwood. The eighth piece does not show the sameness of the others and therefore, I would conclude that Perry is not the author of it." Dr. Lincoln clicked her laser pointer. "This is the one that does not belong."

The suicide letter showed on the board ... it was the one that did not fit.

Angie moved her hand to her mouth. "Perry didn't write the note?"

"I believe he did not."

The chief asked, "Would you feel comfortable testifying in court about these findings?"

"Yes, I would," Dr. Lincoln said. "You see here and here?" The woman used the light of the pointer to circle several words on the screen. "This is not how Perry communicated. Phrases and constructions like these are not seen in his writing."

"Then the note was written by someone other than Perry." Courtney stated for clarification.

"That's correct."

"The author of that note put it together trying to make us believe that Perry took his own life." Angie's cheeks turned pink with anger and she turned to look at her sister. "If Courtney hadn't pointed out the note's differences, then we'd all think Perry had killed himself."

"Most likely." Dr. Lincoln gave a nod and made eye contact with Courtney. "What made you think the note was written by someone else?"

Courtney said, "I took a linguistics course in college. I thought it was fascinating. The professor gave a lecture on syntax and words and contrasted the language used in several pieces of correspondence. It was clear the classroom examples were not written by the same person. I wondered about the way this note was written. From what I'd heard about Perry, I didn't think the note was written by him. It didn't sound like something he would put together." Courtney left out the part about how her paranormal skills might have had something to do with making the observation.

"You're very perceptive," Dr. Lincoln said with an admiring smile.

"Are you able to give us any clues about the person who might have written the false suicide note?" Chief Martin asked.

"The person who wrote this is probably very intelligent. He or she has command of higher-level vocabulary and syntax," Dr. Lincoln told them. "I made two observations ... the writer might be an older person as some turns of phrase seem more akin to an older writing style ... *or* the writer may just have a difficult time switching from formal language to informal language. Either way, from analysis of the seven other writing samples, I believe the author of this note did *not* do a good job of trying to sound like Perry."

"I never met Perry, but after hearing about him and reading that note, I could not believe he took his own life," Courtney said, her eyes flashing. "Someone killed him and then tried to make it look like suicide. We all could have fallen for the deception and then the killer would have gotten away with it."

"Are there any hints in the writing that tell you if the author is male or female?" Chief Martin asked.

"Unfortunately, not in this case."

After fifteen more minutes of questions and answers, it was clear there would not be any hints or clues as to who the killer might be so Angie, Courtney, and the chief thanked Dr. Lincoln for all of her help and left the university building and walked towards the parking lot.

"Good work," Angie told her sister. "You were right about Perry not writing the suicide note. Someone killed him."

"Two questions," Courtney said. "Who did it? And why?"

Chief Martin said, "There was no sign of forced entry into the boarding house so either a door was left unlocked, the killer was invited in by someone in the house, or the killer lives in the house. Dr. Lincoln suggests whoever wrote the note might be an older person. There are three people living in the house who are older. Maribeth, Mary Bishop, and Roger Winthrop. Some residents of the house have mentioned that Maribeth was angry at Perry, but it was because he was not helping out around the place. That doesn't seem like a reason to kill. Mary Bishop was friendly with Perry, she admitted to occasionally helping Perry by filling his syringe for him when his headaches were kicking in. Roger says he and Perry got along well and no one in the house has disagreed with that. If the killer is one of those three people, then we need to figure out what was behind the motivation to kill."

They stood next to the chief's car in the lot.

The talk of murder brought the sights and sounds of the early morning when they were summoned inside to Perry's room back into Angie's mind, and for a few moments, she was a million miles away reliving the experience. The smell that floated on the air that day flickered in Angie's senses and caused her stomach to lurch.

Taking a deep breath, she shook herself and brought her attention back to the conversation. "Dr. Lincoln also told us the person who wrote the note may be someone who can't switch easily to informal speech. Who have we met fits that description?"

Courtney said, "Perry's former girlfriend, Maura Norris, could come off that way. You said it seemed hard for her to relax."

"Charles Conte would fit that description," Chief Martin said. "He was formal and stand-offish when we talked to him. Maybe when he's around friends he's able to use more everyday language, but he showed no inclination to do so when we had a chat with him."

Opening the car door, Angie gave a half-smile. "Looks like we've got our work cut out for us."

17

The sisters buzzed around the kitchen preparing picnic dinners for themselves and for some of the bed and breakfast guests who had plans to attend the summer solstice celebration on the town common. The popular annual event showcased multiple bands that would be playing on the bandstand through the evening and into the night.

Tourists and townspeople brought lawn chairs and blankets and carried their own dinners in coolers or baskets, or bought food from the food trucks that parked at one end of the common. It was always a festive way to officially kick off summer and the Roselands and Mr. Finch never missed it.

Finch stood at the kitchen counter assembling

the potato salad while Angie frosted several flavors of cupcakes. Courtney had a long French bread loaf resting on the island to which she added sliced seasoned chicken, cheese, tomatoes, onions, arugula, pickles, and the homemade dressing, and then sliced the loaf into small sub sandwiches. She'd already completed a vegetarian loaf for those who preferred not to eat meat, and next up, was the Italian meats and cheeses option.

Ellie prepared the yogurt and fruit by lining up the small cups, spooning granola into the bottom third, layering in the yogurt, adding the sliced strawberries and blueberries, and then topping with a dollop of whipped cream.

When Angie had finished frosting the cupcakes, she frosted the pans of the everything-brownies and then sprinkled the chopped up cookies, pretzels, and peanut butter cups over the top. After placing them in the refrigerator for ten minutes to set, she used a sharp knife to cut the brownies into squares and then wrapped them individually with cellophane.

Ellie removed the wicker picnic baskets from the storage closet and began packing them with the food and cold packs. When they were done, she and Courtney carried the four B and B guests' baskets to the side table in the dining room for easy pickup.

"Okay, everything's ready." Ellie took in a long breath. "We can head to the common."

Finch's girlfriend, Betty, drove up to the Victorian right on time and the sisters packed her trunk with the goodies, blankets, and folding chairs while Betty walked around the car to help Mr. Finch maneuver himself into the front passage seat.

"What a handsome man," Betty cooed over Finch. "You look very nice in your new shirt." The real estate agent could have an abrupt, slightly hard edge to her, but she was sweet and loving to the older man who had stolen her heart.

Finch's cheeks turned pink and a wide smile spread over his face.

"That's everything." Angie closed the back doors and the trunk. "We'll meet you at the common to get everything out of the car. We're going to walk. Just leave the things in the car until we get there."

"Oh, there's Euclid in the window." Finch leaned out the car window and waved to the big orange cat. "I hope he isn't insulted that we're not taking him and Circe along."

As Betty went back to the driver's seat, she said, "For land's sake, Victor, they're cats. They don't get insulted."

Angie and Finch exchanged knowing looks and

she said softy, "I explained to them that they wouldn't like the noise of the bands performing. They seemed happy to have the house to themselves for the evening."

Betty and Finch drove off just as Josh pulled into the driveway of the Victorian in his shiny red roadster. "Sorry I'm late." He gave Angie a kiss and dashed into the house to change.

Jack and Rufus walked down the street and onto the front lawn at the same time Tom came up the road from his and Jenna's house. When everyone had assembled, they headed one block to the town's charming and picturesque Main Street that would lead down to the common.

Earlier in the day, Angie and Josh took part in the annual summer solstice 10k run which wound through town, down to Coveside, along the ocean bluffs, to the edge of Silver Cove, and then back to the finish line near the common. Despite having little time to prepare and wanting to do the race for the fun of enjoying the morning with the townsfolk and to support a charitable cause, they were both pleased with their finishing times.

Once at the common, the group found Betty's car, removed the items, and set up their things on the sweet lush grass of the common to the left of the bandstand and then dug into the food as the sun lowered in the pink and violet sky.

Everyone shared bits about their workdays, and Angie and Courtney reported on the trip to the university to meet with the expert on forensic linguistics.

"I never knew there was such a specialty." Rufus bit into a brownie before dipping his spoon into the fruit and yogurt parfait.

"So the professor believes the note was *not* written by Perry Wildwood," Jack repeated what the sisters told him. "It makes sense since the syringe was never found. I don't think any of us thought Perry killed himself after hearing what the man was like."

Courtney reported that Dr. Lincoln believed the author of the note was either an older person or someone who spoke and wrote in a more formal way.

"From what you've told us," Tom said, "there are three older people who live in the house."

Sitting together on the blanket, Jenna leaned against her husband as she finished her sandwich. "And there are two people who could be considered more formal in their speech patterns ... Maura Norris and Charles Conte, Perry's friend."

Courtney said, "None of us have met Charles, but Angie and I are going to the police station tomorrow to sit in when Chief Martin talks to Charles again."

"Law enforcement did not find any evidence of an intruder so the person responsible for Perry's death either entered the home through an unlocked door or is a resident of the house," Angie pointed out.

"Or," Ellie said, "was a guest who was let in by a resident."

"That narrows suspects down somewhat," Josh said. "Did any of the residents admit to having a guest?"

"Everyone denies it," Jenna said.

"Then that leaves only one person who might have had a friend or acquaintance over ... Perry," Mr. Finch said.

"And he's unable to tell you anything," Betty said as she finished her sandwich.

"Nobody heard anything and nobody saw anything," Rufus said. "Is that hard to believe?"

"I guess not," Angie said. "It's a big house. Everyone has rooms on the second floor except for Perry and Megan Milton. If a friend arrived later in the evening, the other residents were probably asleep at that time."

Courtney said, "Charles was at the boarding house to borrow a book on the night Perry was killed. He doesn't remember what time he was there. He told Chief Martin he always loses track of time. I don't believe him."

The discussion about Perry's death ended when the first band took the stage and began to play. Tom and Josh stood up to speak with a businessman they knew, Courtney and Rufus rested side by side on the blanket, Jack and Ellie strolled around the common, and Finch and Betty held hands sitting next to each other in lawn chairs while tapping their toes to the beat of the music.

Angie and Jenna decided to walk to a food truck for some hot tea and on the way, they ran into their friend, Francine, an attractive blonde with emerald green eyes who ran the stained glass shop in town.

"How are things with the new boyfriend?" Angie asked.

Francine's eyes twinkled. "Everything is just great. Edgar went to get us some ice cream sundaes."

After talking about what was new with each of them, the conversation turned to the murder of the young man at the boarding house.

"How can a murder happen with other people in the place?" Francine asked. "Nobody noticed or heard a struggle or an argument?"

Angie shrugged. "It seems not."

A frown tugged at Francine's lips. "I walked by the boarding house a couple of weeks ago. It was early evening. I was delivering a stained glass piece to the restaurant down the street."

Angie and Jenna listened with interest wondering why their friend had a look of concern on her face.

"There was a young woman on the wraparound terrace heading towards the front door. A man was behind her. He said something. I couldn't hear the words. The woman turned around to face him. She turned so fast that he almost bashed into her. He said something else and looked like he was going to lean in to kiss her." Francine paused.

"What happened?" Jenna asked.

Francine blinked. "The young woman slapped him across the face. Then she stormed into the house."

"Wow," Angie said.

"Their exchange really bothered me. I hurried by on the other side of the street. It was dusk. There are a lot of shade trees on that road. Neither one of them saw me. The interaction shook me up." Francine shuddered recalling the incident.

"What did the guy do after the woman went inside?" Jenna asked.

"He walked down the steps and headed in the direction I had come from."

"What did the woman look like?" Angie asked, her heart pounding.

"She looked to be in her mid-twenties, auburn hair to the shoulders. Fit looking, pretty."

"What about the man?" Angie asked.

Francine said, "He was tall. Late twenties, maybe? Very light blond hair. Sort of gawky looking. I wouldn't describe him as athletic. He moved a little awkwardly, a little uncoordinated, like he'd never played a sport in his life."

"How did he react when the woman slapped him?" Jenna asked.

"It was almost like he had no reaction at all. He stared at her until she disappeared into the house, then he walked away."

"Did he give the impression he was angry?"

"No, I wouldn't say that. He seemed sort of ... resigned? Not quite that. He almost gave the impression that it was a setback, but he wasn't going to give up. Like I said, the whole thing lasted a minute. It's the impression I got." Francine rubbed at the side of her face. "Something about the whole thing seemed ... ominous? I was upset by it. I couldn't shake it off until I went to bed that night. I know it's foolishness, but when I heard someone died in the boarding house, I have to say I wasn't a bit surprised that something bad had happened in there."

harles Conte was tall, thin, and gangly with nearly white blond hair and brown eyes. He was almost thirty, but his long, lean look and the way he moved his body made him seem almost a teenager. In addition to his awkward physical appearance, he was awkward socially, not always making eye contact when it was appropriate, sometimes taking a long time to answer questions, responding in a blunt, almost impolite manner.

Before Charles arrived at the police station, Chief Martin gave Angie and Courtney a brief overview of the man. "Mr. Conte is considered by many to be brilliant, a genius. His plan is to become a neurosurgeon, although the medical school instructors have encouraged him to go into research. They think Conte will win the Nobel Prize one day."

"Wow." Courtney's eyes widened. "Seriously?"

The chief went on. "Conte skipped a grade, seemingly has the ability to look at material and know it within minutes. His teachers felt he never had to try in class. Science and medicine come very easily to him. Social skills do not come easily, however. He can come off as abrasive, not a team player, downright rude, but is oblivious as to why people think such things about him."

Angie pushed at a pencil on the table. "Behavior like that can lead to a lot of trouble."

"Indeed, it can." The chief went out to the lobby and brought the gifted, talented future doctor into the conference room.

"Why do I need to talk to you again?" Charles asked the chief as he looked from person to person.

"We often speak to people multiple times," Chief Martin said. "It can be very helpful to us."

Charles asked why the two young women were present and Courtney explained their roles as consultants to the police department.

"What are your qualifications?" Charles asked.

Courtney stared him down with a wilting look

and said, "We aren't allowed to discuss that. It's classified information."

Charles blinked several times while processing what Courtney had said. He didn't ask a follow-up question.

"Have you had a chance to think back on your visit to Perry on the night he died?" Chief Martin asked. "Have you been able to recall the time you made the visit to the boarding house?"

"No," was all Charles said in reply.

"What about a time frame?"

"Between sunset and sunrise."

If anyone else responded in that way, the chief would have been sure the person was being flip and antagonistic, but that's not the way Charles came across. His answers seemed sincere and without ill-intention.

"Please repeat for us why you went to see Perry that night, what happened when you were inside the boarding house, and how long you stayed," Chief Martin requested.

Charles let out a soft sigh and gave a slight shrug. "Certainly." He cleared his throat. "I know Perry from the medical school. We've been in classes and rotations together. There are times when we share information, books, articles, clips of presentations.

He is very smart and has a talent for medicine." Charles sat very straight in his chair. "Perry had a book I wanted to read. He wasn't done with it, but he knows I'm able to read quite fast and would be able to return it to him the following day."

"What was the book you wanted to borrow?" Chief Martin asked.

Charles gave a long title that had something to do with anesthesia and blood sugar levels during cardiac surgery.

"You went to Perry's to get it?"

"I did."

"What else did you do that night?"

"I was reading in the library. There were a number of articles I wanted to get ahead on," Charles said matter-of-factly.

"Were you in the library before or after seeing Perry?"

"Both."

"Did Perry know you were coming?" the chief asked.

"Yes, as I told you previously, I texted him and he texted me saying to come within the hour."

"Do you still have those texts on your phone?"

"I don't, no. I delete texts after I send and receive them. I do not like clutter."

"If we check with the phone company, they'll be able to confirm that you and Perry texted that night?"

"They will." Charles still sat at attention in his seat. His face was expressionless, but attentive.

From what she'd seen so far, Angie thought it was best that Charles had no interest in becoming a family physician or general practitioner since the man was very robotic and lacked a pleasant bedside manner. She imagined it would be very difficult for Charles to connect with a patient or for him to present a caring, empathetic demeanor.

"What happened when you arrived at the boarding house?"

"I rang the bell and Perry came to open it. We went to his room off the hallway and he gave me the book."

"If Perry knew you were coming, why didn't he just hand the book to you at the door?" Chief Martin asked.

"Perhaps Perry thought I wouldn't arrive until later. I have a habit of becoming engrossed in my work and losing track of time. Perry was aware of this."

"Did you see anyone else in the house when you were there?"

"No one. The house was quiet. I believe the other residents were in their rooms."

"What did you and Perry talk about when you were in his room?" Angie asked.

Charles turned to her with a slight expression of surprise as if he'd forgotten she was in the room. "Perry told me what chapter he'd read in the book. He had a favorable opinion of it. I told him I'd give it back to him when I saw him in the lab the next day."

"Did you talk about anything else?" Angie questioned.

"Just the book."

"Did you stay for a little while? Did you sit down?" Courtney asked.

"There was no reason to. I left the house and returned to the library."

Angie asked with a pleasant tone of voice, "How did Perry seem when you were with him?"

"How do you mean?"

"Did he seem tired? Happy? Energetic? Did he seem like he wasn't feeling well?"

"He seemed normal."

"What was normal for Perry?" Angie asked.

Charles looked down at the table thinking about the question. "Perry was like he usually was. Nice.

Helpful. He made intelligent, insightful comments about the book."

"Did you like Perry?"

"Most of the time."

"When *didn't* you like him?"

Charles pursed his lips. "When I was busy or when we disagreed about something or if I was late and he got angry about it."

"Did you argue?" the chief asked.

"Not exactly. We didn't get into fights or yelling matches. We just annoyed one another sometimes. We had different viewpoints and defended them. Neither one of us liked to be thought of as wrong or misinformed."

"What was Perry doing when you left?" Angie asked.

"He walked me to the front door and said good-bye. I left and he closed the door behind me. I don't know what he did after that."

Angie decided to come out with the question she wanted to ask. "Did Perry have a headache that night?"

"I don't know. He didn't mention it to me."

"Did you know Perry had to deal with severe headaches?" Angie asked.

"I knew he got headaches fairly frequently," Charles said.

"Do you know how he treated them?"

"He used an injectable medication that is not approved for headache use."

"Do you think Perry did wrong to use that medication?"

"Some medications are effective for treating conditions they have not been approved for," Charles said.

"But do you think Perry was doing wrong by self-injecting the medication?" Angie asked more specifically.

"No, I don't."

"Why not?"

"It isn't illegal to use something that hasn't yet been approved to treat pain. There are guidelines. Perry followed them."

"But Perry was still a student. He shouldn't have been acquiring medication and treating himself with it. Am I wrong about that?" Angie asked.

Charles said, "In general, you are not wrong, however, if someone wanted to file on Perry, it is my opinion that Perry would not be disciplined for what he was doing."

Angie nodded. "Do you know the other residents of the boarding house?"

"I've met them."

"All of them?"

"At one time or another, I believe."

"Do you know Andy Hobbs?" Courtney asked.

"A poor excuse for a human being."

Angie had to bite her lip to keep from smiling at the comment.

"Why do you say that?" Courtney asked.

"The man is full of himself, rude, self-possessed. He likes to make comments to rile a person and then plays the victim when the person calls him on it."

"Have you ever argued with Andy?" Chief Martin asked.

Charles snorted. "I wouldn't argue with Andy. I don't like to waste my time. He is no match for me mentally or verbally. I'd crush him and he would be humiliated."

Angie's eyebrows shot up her forehead.

"I see," the chief said.

"Do you know Megan Milton?" Angie asked.

"Yes, I do. She's a pharmacy student at the university and a friend of Perry's. She lives in the boarding house," Charles said.

"What do you think of Megan?" Courtney asked.

Charles shifted his eyes to the young woman. "Megan is a very nice person."

"Have you asked her out?"

"Yes."

"Where did you go?"

"Megan declined my invitation."

"Did that upset you?" Courtney asked.

"No. I assumed that it was an inconvenient time for her."

"Have you asked her out again?"

"Just the one time."

"I heard someone say they saw Megan strike you one day on the boarding house porch," Angie said.

Charles shifted a little in his chair and his straight posture sagged slightly. "It happened, yes. I said something to her that she didn't like."

"What did you say to her?" Chief Martin gave the man a serious expression.

"I don't recall."

"You don't have to repeat exactly what you said," Angie told him. "What was the gist of it?"

"I told Megan how beautiful she was and that I would like to kiss her."

"And she hit you?"

Charles nodded.

"Had you said something like that to her before that day?" Angie asked.

"A few times."

"If Megan reacts in a negative way towards you, why do you persist?"

Charles raised an eyebrow. "Because I think she'll change her mind."

Angie stared at the man marveling at how someone could be so incredibly intelligent yet so completely clueless.

19

"Thanks for talking to me again." Angie and Megan Milton sat on the bench on the veranda and looked out over the ocean. "Can you tell me about Charles Conte?"

Megan looked sideways at Angie. "I don't know much about him. Perry told me he's a genius and he knows everything about medicine. Perry said Charles could be difficult, a real pain sometimes, but he liked the guy even though he was odd."

"Do you think he's odd?"

"Yeah. He always seems engrossed in his own thoughts, in his own world. He doesn't seem to care about anyone else. Charles misses a lot of social cues."

"Isn't that a bad thing for a doctor?" Angie asked.

"Perry said Charles's social deficits wouldn't really have an impact on his career because he would choose a very specialized field where only his skill as a doctor would matter."

"I guess that makes sense," Angie said. "Did Perry and Charles do things together?"

"They'd go out for a bite to eat, sometimes go down to the beach, or go see a documentary. Perry told me you had to overlook Charles's quirks and see him for who he was," Megan said. "Perry was right, but I didn't have any interest in getting to know him."

"Perry and Charles had arguments sometimes?"

"Sometimes. Charles could get very angry with Perry when they disagreed about diseases, treatments, and outcomes. Their discussions could get quite heated. I'd shut my door whenever I heard one of their debates starting."

"We've heard that Charles was here at the boarding house the night Perry died," Angie said.

"Oh?"

"Did you run into him in the house?"

"No, I don't think I saw him that evening," Megan said.

"Charles came to see Perry, but he only stayed for a few minutes before leaving. Maybe you were out?"

"I think so."

Something about Megan's answers caused a flicker of doubt to flash through Angie and she shifted on the bench to face her. "Did you happen to run into Charles that night? Maybe somewhere in the neighborhood?"

Megan opened her mouth to speak, but then stopped and took in a breath. "I remember now. I did run into him. He'd been at the house to get a book from Perry. He was heading back to the library."

"You chatted with him?" Angie asked.

"Briefly." Megan looked down at the porch floor. "Look, I don't like the guy. I try to steer clear of him."

"Because he likes you?"

Megan whirled and stared at Angie. "Did you talk to him? Did he tell you that?"

Angie nodded.

Megan leaned back against the bench and sighed loudly. "It's ridiculous. He can't get it through his head that I'm never going to date him. Never. I've spelled it out on several occasions, but it goes in one ear and out the other. Actually, I don't know if it ever goes in his ear. Charles has a mental block against things he doesn't want to hear. It's like he's got a force field around him and only things he wants to hear are acknowledged ... everything else gets ignored."

"He's tried to kiss you?" Angie asked.

"Oh, brother. He told you that?"

"Sort of."

Megan shrugged. "I slapped him one day. I'm ashamed I handled it that way. It was the third or fourth time he came at me for a kiss, and I'd had it. Really, I'm not interested in him and I never will be. There's nothing Charles can do to change my mind."

"Did you tell him that?"

"A thousand times." Megan rolled her eyes. "A million times. I told him we're not the right fit. I told him he is *not* my type."

"What did he say to that?" Angie asked.

"He asked me who was my type."

"How did you answer?"

Megan's shoulders drooped. "I said Perry. Perry was my type. I know that was a stupid thing to say. Charles seemed hurt. I should have picked some celebrity out the air. Or I shouldn't have answered at all. It just came out before I could think."

"Did Charles appear angry?" Angie asked.

"Not angry. Maybe a little sad."

Angie tilted her head to the side. "You saw

Charles outside the boarding house? In the neighborhood? The night Perry died?"

"Yeah." Megan nodded. "About a block from the house."

"Did Charles have anything with him?"

"A book. He said he borrowed a book from Perry."

Angie's eyes widened. "What time was it when you ran into him?"

"I don't know. I went to Main Street to walk around, do a little shopping," Megan said. "I ran into a friend and we went to a restaurant to have a drink together. It was probably a little before midnight?"

"Is the medical school library open after midnight?" Angie asked.

"It's open twenty-four hours a day."

"Okay. Charles said he was returning to the library after picking up the book."

"Not a surprise," Megan said. "Charles practically lives in the library."

Angie couldn't help the look of impatience on her face. "Why didn't you tell us this earlier?"

Megan held her hands up in a helpless gesture. "I don't like talking about Charles. He's a pain."

"When you got home that night, did you see Perry?"

"Just for a few seconds. When I went to my room, Perry was about to shut his door. He said he was tired and was turning in," Megan said.

"Did you tell the police you ran into Charles leaving the house?"

"No. What does it matter if I didn't tell anyone I ran into Charles that night? It doesn't have anything to do with Perry."

Angie tried to keep her frustration out of her voice. "It matters because Charles might have been a suspect. It matters because it proves Perry was alive after Charles left the house. It tells us Perry was alive at midnight."

"Oh." Megan shifted her gaze to her hands. "I didn't think. I should have said something."

"When you saw Perry, did he mention he wasn't feeling well?"

"No. He just said he was tired."

"Did you stay up or did you go right to bed?" Angie asked.

"I went to bed. I was feeling exhausted, like maybe I was coming down with a cold."

"Did you wake up during the night?"

"I don't think so. I didn't get out of bed until I heard the commotion in the morning."

"Did you hear anything that night? Anything

that might have woken you?"

"I don't remember hearing anything at all. If I did wake up from a noise, it didn't register with me and I must have fallen back to sleep," Megan said.

~

AFTER LEAVING MEGAN, Angie met Chief Martin at the police station to tell him what she'd learned.

"That throws cold water on my train of thought." The chief absent-mindedly twirled his pen between his fingers. "After talking with Charles Conte the second time, my suspicions about him grew. It sounds like he has a temper and has argued with Perry on a number of occasions. It seemed plausible that Charles could strike out at Perry during an argument. He knew Perry used an injectable medication for his headaches. He probably knows where the medication and syringes are kept in Perry's room. Charles has a thing for Megan."

"And on top of all that," Angie said, "Megan told Charles that Perry is her type and Charles is not."

"Right," the chief said. "Now there's only one problem with suspecting Charles."

Angie nodded. "Perry was alive after Charles left the boarding house."

"Yup." Chief Martin ran his hand over his face. "We're coming up empty. Nobody saw anything. Nobody heard anything." Leaning back in his chair, he asked, "Do you *feel* anything about this case? About anyone in particular?"

Angie's sensations were a big, messy jumble that swirled around and around and wouldn't come together in a logical way. "That smell in Perry's room still picks at me. I know only Jenna and I could smell it, and because of that I think it points to the killer. Unfortunately, *how* and *who* is beyond me so far." Angie looked across the room at nothing. "I also think someone in that house knows more than they're telling us. Maybe Megan ... maybe Mary Bishop. They were both close to Perry. Why would someone keep information from us? Is the person trying to protect someone? Is the person afraid of someone? Was the person threatened into silence? Is the person the only one who knows something incriminating and if he or she tells us, the killer will retaliate?" Angie's forehead creased in thought. "Is there another reason someone wouldn't share important information with us?"

Chief Martin asked, "Because that person is the killer?"

20

Angie, Jenna, Mr. Finch, and Ellie emptied the contents of the bags onto the counter of the boarding house while Maribeth exclaimed over each dish. In a kind gesture, the sisters and Finch had prepared dinner for Maribeth and the residents of the boarding house so everyone could relax, enjoy a good meal, and talk.

"This is bowtie pasta in a cheese sauce and this pan holds the same pasta but in a red sauce," Ellie pointed.

"We have grilled vegetables in this one," Jenna said, "and this pan has meatballs and sausages."

Angie peeled back the foil on another pan. "This one has the mixed green salad and that one over by the refrigerator has the garlic bread in it."

"What a feast." Closing her eyes and inhaling the delicious odors, Maribeth smiled from ear to ear. "I'm sorry Courtney couldn't make it."

Finch said, "She's minding the candy shop this evening."

"Well, please thank her, too. I know she pitched in to help make the food," Maribeth said. "It's such a treat not to have to make the evening meal. The residents will love this. Thank you so much.

"And we'll clean up afterwards, too," Jenna assured the woman while taking the white plates from the cabinet and heading to the dining room to set the table. "It will give you a little break."

"Speaking of enjoying a little break," Finch winked as he opened a bottle of wine and poured some into a few glasses.

"Oh, gosh." When Maribeth saw the wine, she put her hand over her heart. "I'd better not."

"Nonsense." Finch handed Maribeth one of the stemmed glasses. "This is an evening to relax with friends."

"Well, I guess I could." Maribeth accepted the wine. "But just a little."

"That's the spirit." Finch clinked his glass against hers as Roger Winthrop and Mary Bishop entered the kitchen and headed for the island.

"You brought wine, too? How wonderful." Roger helped himself and then asked, "Mary? A glass?"

Mary nodded and sipped. "Oh, it's lovely."

The platters and pans were placed in the ovens to keep the meal warm and the rest of the residents began to arrive from their rooms to enjoy drinks and hors d'oeuvres of smoked salmon crisps, bruschetta, mini potato latkes, puff pastry squares with fig preserves and stilton cheese, and French fries with chive sour cream.

Megan came in to join the group and Andy Hobbs showed up a few minutes later.

"Look at all this." Andy swallowed a salmon crisp. "I wouldn't mind if you Roselands and Mr. Finch were here every night if this was the result."

Megan started a conversation with Mary and Maribeth, while Roger carried a small plate of food over to stand beside Finch. The three sisters moved around the room mingling with the others and it didn't take long before everyone was feeling comfortable and the chatter began to flow.

Jenna said, "Isn't it interesting that everyone who lives in the house works or studies in a medical field."

"I guess that's true," Mary said. "I was an accountant for years, but now I work part time in a doctor's office."

"I don't know if that counts," Andy said.

"Of course it counts," Maribeth replied. "Mary does billing so she has to know and understand medical terms and codes to do her work correctly."

"Understanding *terms* isn't equivalent to *medical* understanding," Andy said.

Megan gave Andy the eye. "Jenna pointed out that we all work or study in a medical environment. We all do. Even Mary."

Andy was about to open his mouth in protest when Roger clapped him on the shoulder. "No need to split hairs. You're making unnecessary distinctions. It's not important."

Andy huffed and reached for several potato latkes. "I think it *is* important to be precise in the use of language."

"We're not in the classroom," Roger said. "We're socializing."

Mary sidled up to Angie and sighed. "I don't know why Andy has to be so antagonistic. It can make people want to avoid him."

"Is he often like that?" Angie asked.

"Often enough. You never know what you'll get with Andy," Mary said. "He can be very quiet at times and then he can be challenging and contrary. Whatever is said, he wants to take the opposite position." The woman shook her head. "Doesn't he see the effect he has on other people? He turns people off. They don't want to be around him. Why would he want to do that?"

"Some people are like that," Angie said. "I don't think it can be explained."

"Maybe they like drama," Mary suggested. "Maybe they don't like it when things are going smoothly. Anyway, *I* don't like it when he behaves that way." Mary moved off to get more appetizers.

Megan came up next to Angie. "Any news about Perry? Are the police close to figuring out what happened?"

"I don't know," Angie said. "I hope so."

Wearing a sad expression on her face, Megan said, "It seems so odd when I pass by Perry's room. I can't believe he's gone. He had so much to live for, so many plans." She had to stop speaking as her throat tightened and the words wouldn't come out.

Angie gave Megan's shoulder a squeeze of sympathy knowing that the young woman's grief was for more than losing a friend and housemate. Trying to think of something comforting to say, Angie's brain came up empty ... nothing was enough to counter such loss.

Megan ran her hand across her face. "Anyway, the police will discover the killer. They'll find him eventually."

"Have you remembered anything new about the night?" Angie asked.

"Nothing." The corners of Megan's lips tugged down. "It must have been quick. The attacker went into Perry's room, prepared the injection, and gave it to him. The medication is so fast-acting Perry didn't have a chance to react. He probably didn't know what was happening."

"Really? It's that fast?" Angie knew the medication was swift, but she didn't fully comprehend just how fast it could take someone's life.

"Seconds," Megan said softly. "At overdose levels, it would only take about four to six seconds."

"The killer must have known what he was doing," Angie said. "He must have known Perry would be dead almost before the last drops of medication entered his body."

"I'm sure he did."

Angie turned the conversation to a different topic. "Have you run into Charles lately?"

A look of disgust instantly took over the sad

expression that had seemed at home on Megan's face. "No, I haven't."

"Has he tried to get in touch with you?"

Megan narrowed her eyes. "How would he? He doesn't know my number."

"It would be easy to find your number," Angie said.

"It's unlisted," Megan said defensively.

"You haven't seen Charles at the university?"

"Not today. Not yesterday. But I'm sure I'll run into him someday soon." Megan gave a weary shrug. "I don't want to see him."

Angie asked, "What time did you say you ran into Charles on the night Perry died?"

"Around midnight. Why?" Megan cocked her head to the side.

"I'm helping the police with the timeline. I need to be sure everything is accurate," Angie said.

"Yeah," Megan said, "it was midnight, or right around that time."

"When you were going into the house, did you notice what direction Charles went?"

"I don't think I noticed," Megan said. "He wasn't behind me and that was all I cared about."

Mary came over to the young women to join in

with whatever they were discussing. "What are you talking about?" she asked with interest.

"Oh, just this and that," Angie said with smile.

"Mostly about Perry?" Mary asked.

"Mostly," Megan told her. "I think I'm going to get myself a cold drink."

Mary took a step closer to Angie. "I want to talk to you. Would you come up to my room?"

"Sure," Angie said trying to figure out why Mary suddenly wanted her on the second floor, and she didn't think the reason was because it was quieter up there.

Angie followed after Mary as they entered the elevator and pushed the buttons on the control panel.

In contrast to her friendly and outgoing personality, Mary didn't say much on the ride up to the next floor and when the slow-as-molasses elevator finally deposited them on the upper floor, Mary brought Angie to the sitting room of her suite.

"I wanted to bring something up with you." Mary's face looked a little pale. "I haven't mentioned this to anyone."

Angie's senses went on high alert ... her head began to buzz.

"It's about the night Perry passed away," Mary

said. "You asked me a few days ago if I'd heard anything unusual in the house. You didn't ask me if I'd *seen* something unusual. Which I did."

"What was it?" A flush of nervousness raced through Angie's body.

"I was sitting on my bed by the window that night," Mary said. "I had some sewing to do, but I was feeling sleepy and decided to put the things away. I gathered everything up and got off the bed to go to the other side of the room."

Angie encouraged the woman to continue.

"As I was passing the window, I thought I saw someone in the yard by the backdoor. I turned off my lamp and tip-toed to other side of the window to get a better view."

"Did you see Perry out there?"

"No, not Perry. I saw two people. I couldn't hear what they were talking about. One of them was Andy Hobbs."

"Andy?" Angie asked. "Could you see who the other person was?"

"The other person was in shadow. I couldn't see the face. I couldn't tell if it was a man or a woman."

"Did Andy and the other person show up at the same time?"

"I don't know," Mary said. "I only saw them when they were already standing at the rear door."

"Did they come into the house?" Angie asked, her eyes wide.

"The other person turned around and headed out of the yard. The yard was dark, full of shadows." Mary leaned closer and spoke softly. "Andy watched the person go, then he reached into his back pocket and took out his key."

"Andy came inside the house?"

"Yes, but before he did, Andy returned his key to his pocket and turned around to look to the rear of the yard. I followed his gaze, but I couldn't see anything. Maribeth keeps a house key near the faucet at the back of the house, in case one of us forgets ours or gets locked out. There's a loose shingle there. The key is hidden under the shingle."

"What's the hidden key got to do with Andy?" Angie asked.

"Andy went to get the key. He unlocked the back door, then he put the key back in its place by the faucet and went inside."

"Maybe Andy had the wrong key in his pocket?" Angie suggested.

"Maybe. But I don't think so," Mary said. "I got

the impression he didn't want to use his own key to get into the house."

Angie's mind raced. "What time was this?"

"Around 12:30. I looked at my alarm clock." Mary said, "Don't tell Andy I saw him that night. He'll know it was me who told you. He knows my room looks out over the rear yard. Andy has a difficult personality. His attitude makes me nervous sometimes."

"I won't tell him," Angie promised.

Mary let out a worried sigh. "Like I said, I couldn't hear what Andy and the other person were saying and I don't know why Andy put his own key back in his pocket, but don't you think there's something odd about the whole thing?"

Yes. Yes, I do.

21

"Tom was right about putting a kitchen in the apartment." Angie pushed the long, loose sleeve of her robe back as she removed an apple pie from the oven and set it on the counter to cool.

"Tom knows what he's doing. I'm glad we took his suggestion. It's nice to have this private space for ourselves." Josh had on navy blue pajama pants and a faded short-sleeved t-shirt.

The young couple had only moved into their new apartment on the upper floor of the Victorian several weeks ago, but it already felt comfortable and homey to them.

While Josh took out a half gallon of vanilla ice cream from the freezer, Angie made tea and carried the mugs to the bedroom where she placed one on each bedside table. "Don't touch the hot mugs," she warned the two cats who were curled in the middle of the bed.

Returning to the small kitchen, Angie asked Josh, "Do you want to wait for the pie to cool a little longer?"

Josh smiled broadly. "No, I want to eat it right now. I love warm apple pie."

After Angie cut and plated two slices and Josh scooped balls of ice cream from the carton and placed one on top of each slice, they carried their dessert to the bedroom, climbed in under the covers as the cats adjusted their positions to accommodate the people. Euclid stretched his long, furry body over Josh's lap causing the man to laugh.

"You don't make it easy to enjoy my pie." Josh held his plate over the huge orange feline's head.

Circe snuggled next to Angie and the young woman held out a fingertip she'd dipped in the melting ice cream so the cat's little pink tongue could lick it.

"Nothing like being alone in our own apart-ment," Josh grinned.

"It's rare that anyone is ever alone in this family."

Angie shook her head as she brought a bite of pie to her mouth.

"It's just the way I want it. I only have my brother and we don't see a lot of each other anymore. I love this big, wacky family."

While Circe trilled and gave Josh a look of contentment, Angie leaned over and gave her new husband a kiss. "It's a good thing you love the family because now you're stuck with us."

"I wouldn't have it any other way," Josh said reaching for his mug being careful not to spill any of the hot liquid onto the cat in his lap.

After finishing their desserts, Josh ran his hand over Euclid's orange fur and listened to his purring before bringing up the case. "Tell me what happened at the boarding house."

Angie took in a long, slow breath and told him what she'd learned from Mary Bishop.

"Do you think the other person in the yard might be a friend of Andy Hobbs?" Josh asked.

"It's possible. But why would he or she walk Andy to the backdoor and leave? Why not go their separate ways to their own places?"

"Maybe they were engrossed in conversation and didn't want to stop talking?" Josh suggested.

"Maybe," Angie said. "Mary got the impression

that Andy didn't want to use his own key to enter the house. Why wouldn't he want to use his key? There isn't a monitor on the lock or on the door logging the residents' comings and goings. What would it matter if he used his own key?"

"Tell me again how Mary Bishop described the incident." Josh leaned his head back on his pillow and closed his eyes as he listened to Angie's retelling, and when she finished, he opened his eyelids. "Andy looked back to the rear of the yard right before he put his key back in his pocket?"

"That's what Mary said," Angie nodded.

"Was he trying to show the person he was with where the spare key was?" Josh asked.

Angie's eyebrows shot up. "You think the person Andy had been with was watching him from the back of the yard?" The young woman slipped out of the bed and started pacing around the room. "And Andy was showing him or her where the key to the house was hidden?"

"Possibly," Josh said.

"But why do that? Why not just tell the person where the key was?" Angie asked.

"I don't know," Josh said. "I guess it was a silly idea."

"I don't think it *is* a silly idea. I think you're right.

I think Andy was showing the other person where the key was. What was the reason though? Why didn't he just tell the person where it was?" Angie's face paled and she hurried to the bed and slipped in next to Josh. "The person at the back of the yard is the killer."

"You think so?"

"There was no sign of forced entry," Angie said excitedly. "That's because the person used the spare key to get in. Andy didn't tell the person where it was because he didn't want to implicate himself as an accomplice. He can claim he never told the killer about the key. He can't be blamed for any of it."

"You think Andy and this other person were in on the murder together?" Josh asked.

"It seems like it." Angie's eyes narrowed showing she was deep in thought. "But something doesn't seem right. Something about it seems off."

"Maybe it will come to you. Maybe if you talk it over with Chief Martin, things will align and point you in the right direction."

"Who is the other person?" Angie asked. "Is he or she really the one who killed Perry? Maybe I should talk to Andy again."

"Why don't you share the information with the chief. I don't think you should talk to Andy Hobbs alone. Go with Chief Martin, or better yet, let the chief interview Hobbs on his own. Maybe steer clear of the guy. Just in case."

"You're right. I'll talk to the chief." Angie made eye contact with Josh and her voice was hopeful. "This seems like an important break in the case. Maybe this is going to lead somewhere."

"It seems likely," Josh agreed.

"You know, when I was at the boarding house, I felt like things that were unsaid were floating on the air. I think what Mary told me is one of them, but I think there's something else. There's another person in the house who knows something he or she hasn't shared. Maybe more than one person. I need to talk to some of them again."

"Not Andy Hobbs," Josh cautioned.

"Not him. I'll leave him to Chief Martin."

Josh nodded and said, "Why don't we give the case a rest for now and focus on us. We haven't talked about it for a few days and the deadline is coming up to make the decision. What are you thinking about locating a second bake shop in the museum?"

Angie sighed. "I know it's a great opportunity and I've wanted to expand for almost a year now."

"But?" Josh asked.

"But is it the right time to do it?" Angie tucked a loose strand of her hair into her ponytail.

"Why do you think it might not be the right time?"

"Business in the bake shop downstairs is booming. Chief Martin calls on us frequently to help him with cases. I would never want to tell him I didn't have time to help. You know we all want to use our skills for good."

"Even Ellie?" Josh kidded about the reluctant Roseland sister who wished none of them had any powers at all.

Angie smiled. "Even Ellie. She isn't thrilled with this special thing we have, but she understands the responsibility that comes with it."

"No matter how busy you are with the bake shop," Josh said, "you've always had time for the chief and the cases."

"I know that." Angie reached over and took her husband's hand. "But we want to start a family. Will I be able to manage everything when we have a small child in our lives?"

Josh's warm eyes held Angie's. "We can wait on starting a family if you feel like the time isn't right."

Angie tilted her head to the side. "I think there's a little girl who is eager to join all of us. I don't want to keep her waiting." Last Christmas, three spirits came to help keep Angie from danger ... one spirit was from the past, one helper was from the present, and one spirit came from the future, Angie's and Josh's daughter-to-be.

Josh's eyes watered and he said softly. "I think about her every day. I can't wait to meet her."

"Me, too," Angie said. "So no, I don't want to put off starting our family. Can I manage all we have going on and all we will have going on with another bake shop location on top of everything else?"

"Deep down, do you want the second location?" Josh asked.

Angie said, "Yeah, I think I do."

"Then go for it. There are a lot of people around who will help us." Josh chuckled as he slipped his arm around Angie and pulled her close. "We're going to have one heck of a full life together."

22

ngie and Megan filled the box with the clean platters, pans, and plates the Roselands and Mr. Finch used to bring dinner to the boarding house the previous night. Before leaving, they'd placed everything in the dishwasher to run and Angie promised to pick up the dishware the next afternoon.

"I think that's everything," Megan said.

"If you find something else just put it aside and I'll pick it up when I come on Monday to drop off the breakfast baked goods," Angie said. "Where is everyone? The house is so quiet."

"Maribeth is off to a dentist appointment," Megan said. "Mary is at her part-time job, and Roger is tutoring a student at the town library. Andy is always at school at this time. I don't have classes this afternoon. The two new residents aren't moving in for two more weeks." Megan sighed. "It will be strange having someone else living in Perry's room."

"I bet so," Angie said kindly.

"It's also strange not having him around to talk to," Megan said. "I miss him."

Angie put her hand on the young woman's shoulder. "I'm sorry it's been so hard on you."

"Perry's things have been cleared out of his room. Most of the stuff was donated. I took one of his books." Megan shrugged. "I just wanted something that had belonged to him." Slumping against the kitchen island, she asked, "Why can't the police figure this out? Not having an arrest keeps us from having closure. I want to know who killed Perry. I want the person to go to prison. I want it to be over."

Angie wasn't sure Megan would soon find the closure she was hoping for.

"Do you know anything?" Megan asked Angie. "Are the police close to solving this?"

"They don't tell me things like that." Not sure if Megan was in the right mood to talk about what happened, Angie took the chance and asked a question. "Can we talk about the night Perry passed away?"

Megan looked like she'd been hit by something. "What is left to say?"

"How did you come into the house that night? After you ran into Charles, what door did you come in through?"

"The front." Megan's voice sounded slightly sullen.

"And you went right to your rooms?" Angie asked.

"Yes."

"But you saw Perry before going into your suite?"

"I told you that, yeah."

"How did Perry seem?"

"Normal. He said he was tired. He was about to go to bed."

"Was anyone in the room with him?" Angie asked.

Megan's eyes widened. "Like who?"

"A friend? A date?"

Megan's cheeks flushed. "He was alone."

"Are you sure? How do you know that? Was the bedroom door open or closed? Could you see into the bedroom from out in the hall?" Angie questioned.

Blinking fast a few times, Megan's eyes watered and when she started to speak, her voice broke, and she went silent.

"*Was* someone with Perry?" Angie asked.

Megan coughed and cleared her throat. "No one was in his room."

"You're sure?"

"Yes, I'm sure." Megan's arms hung weakly by her sides. "I went into Perry's room before he closed it for the night. We talked for a few minutes. He told me he was really tired and needed to sleep. I asked if his head was hurting. He said it wasn't." Megan stopped talking and looked down at the floor for a minute. "I told Perry I'd make him some tea, if he wanted some. Standing there that night, I was overcome with my feelings for Perry. I blurted out what I felt for him and then I stepped close and kissed him." A few tears escaped from the young woman's eyes and traced down her cheek.

"What did he do?" Angie asked softly.

"He stepped back from me to break off the kiss. I was horrified, so embarrassed. I don't know why I did it."

"Did Perry say anything?"

"He said he was sorry, but he couldn't commit to

a relationship. He wanted to be friends." Megan groaned. "It was such a stupid thing to do. I knew Perry didn't want anything, but I went ahead and kissed him anyway. Ugh. I acted the same way Charles acted with me. I've been disgusted with myself since that night. What's wrong with me?"

"You had feelings for Perry and you acted on them hoping he would feel the same way. There's nothing wrong with you," Angie said.

"I complain about Charles and then I went and did the same thing to Perry," Megan moaned.

"No, it's not the same thing. You and Perry were friends. You don't have any kind of relationship with Charles. And unlike Charles, I don't believe you would ever have kissed Perry again," Angie said.

"I wouldn't have." Megan wiped the tears from her face. "I never would have done that again. It was too painful to be rejected. I don't know if I could have stayed friends with Perry. I was too ashamed of myself."

"He would have stayed friends with you," Angie assured the woman. "Maybe things would have been awkward for a few days, but your friendship would have fallen right back into place, with no harm done to it."

"I hope so."

"What happened after Perry told you he wanted to be friends?"

"I apologized. Over and over. Perry said it was fine and not to be concerned. He said he was going to bed and he'd see me in the morning," Megan said. "I hurried back to my rooms. I went to my bed and sobbed, for a long time. I exhausted myself. I fell asleep and didn't wake up until I heard the commotion out in the hall the next morning."

"Is Perry's room still open?" Angie asked. "Can I go see it for a minute?"

Megan stared at Angie for a few moments and then said, "The door's open. The rooms are empty. The housekeeper is coming next week to give it a final cleaning before the new person moves in."

Angie and Megan walked down the hallway from the kitchen to the two suites at the rear of the house and stopped at the doorway to Perry's former rooms. The space looked sad and lonely with nothing inside but a few dust bunnies on the floor.

Angie took several steps into the sitting room and turned in a circle taking everything in and remembering where Perry's furniture had stood ... she pictured the sofa, the desk, a chair. She looked out of the three windows on the right-side wall.

Suddenly, a sickeningly strong medicinal odor hit Angie hard causing her stomach to roil and her vision to dim. Afraid that movement would make her heave, she stood still, closed her eyes, and took in slow breaths, but the smell was too much and she knew if she stayed in the room, she would surely become sick. Rushing out of the room and into the hall, Angie sucked in long, slow breaths trying to calm herself.

"What's wrong?" Megan asked taking a quick look into the room. "Are you okay?"

"The smell. It makes me feel ill," Angie wheezed.

"What smell?" Megan questioned. "I don't smell anything. What does it smell like?"

Angie wouldn't have been able to describe the odor even if she'd wanted to, and she didn't want to because she remembered that only she and Jenna had been able to sense the smell when they'd been there previously.

"Can we step outside? Is there a door out this way?"

"Yeah. At the end of the hall." Megan led the way, passing a laundry room and a small office on the same side as her suite. Perry's suite was an addition to the house which jutted out on the left side so his sitting room windows looked out to the rear yard.

Unlocking the door, Megan pushed it open so Angie could get out into the fresh air.

Angie sank down on the back steps, holding her head in her hands.

"Can I get you something?" Megan asked. "A glass of water? Some juice?"

"I'll be okay. I just need a minute." Being outside was already making Angie feel much better and the sensation of illness was all but gone. She lifted her head and glanced around the back garden. Benches were placed around the yard under shade trees, a fire pit was set up off to one side, two round tables with umbrellas stood on a stone patio, and a vegetable garden had recently been planted. Tall trees lined the periphery of the property and a pathway led out under an arbor and away from the yard.

"Where does the path go?" Angie asked.

"It splits into two. One way goes down through the rocks to the small beach and the other way leads back to the front of the house."

"What happens when one of the residents gets locked out or they lose their key?" Angie asked.

"Maribeth hid a key in the yard back here," Megan said. "Sorry, but we're not allowed to tell other people where it is ... for security reasons."

Standing up, Angie rubbed at the back of her neck and turned to face the back of the house. She gestured to one of the windows on the second floor. "Is that Mary Bishop's room?"

"Yeah," Megan said. "How did you know?"

"Mary asked me up to her room last night," Angie said. "She wanted to chat privately for a few minutes."

Megan looked hopeful. "Did Mary have anything to say about what happened to Perry? Did she hear something that night?"

"No, she didn't. She only wanted to talk about her concerns regarding house security," Angie said deflecting the question. "Maribeth told me she'll be having a new security system installed soon."

"We all hoped it could have been installed sooner, but the company was backed up," Megan said.

Angie spotted the faucet at the back of the house and walked over to it. She turned it on and splashed water onto her face, and while doing that, she noticed the loose shingle about twelve inches from the spigot.

Touching it with her hand, she pushed the shingle a little to the side and saw the house key hanging from a nail. Megan hadn't seen Angie move the shingle.

Straightening up, Angie said, "There's a loose piece of siding here by the faucet. Maribeth will want to fix it."

"Oh, is there?" Megan asked. "I'll let her know."

23

A ngie received an early morning text from Chief Martin asking if she and one of her sisters or Mr. Finch could meet him at the boarding house. Making sure the bake shop employees could manage the store for a few hours, she and Jenna hurried to meet the chief, speculating all the way to the house about what might have happened.

"Maybe Chief Martin is making an arrest in the case," Jenna's tone was hopeful as she parked the car in the boarding house lot and got out.

Seeing the chief's somber facial expression as he stood on the front porch erased any hope the twin sisters had about the case having been solved.

Climbing the steps, Angie said, "It doesn't seem like you have good news for us."

"You're right." Chief Martin walked the sisters to the side of the porch where seven small mailboxes were set onto the railing. "In the past, there was some minor trouble when the mail to the house got mixed up in one box. Residents took the wrong mail, things got lost, so Maribeth decided to set up the separate mailboxes. That way, each resident has their own mail set in their own boxes. It was a simple thing to do, but it kept people from fussing and blaming others for mixed up mail."

"Is that why you asked us here?" Jenna asked with a cheeky smile. "To show us the mail setup?"

"In part," the chief said. "Something was delivered yesterday to one of the house residents."

Angie's chest tightened. "What was it?"

"A syringe. A syringe full of melathiocaine."

Angie's breath caught. "The same thing that killed Perry."

"It was found in Megan's mailbox," the chief pointed out.

"Was it wrapped in anything?" Jenna asked. "Or was it out in the open?"

"It was underneath some other mail. She could

easily have been pricked by the needle, but it wouldn't have been lethal."

"Megan found it?" Angie asked.

"She did," Chief Martin said. "And was not happy about it."

"You think it's a warning?" Angie asked. "Whoever put it in the box couldn't have thought it would harm Megan. It's probably a message?"

"I had the same idea," the chief said.

"It's awfully bold, isn't it?" Jenna asked. "To put a syringe in the mailbox in a place where a number of people live. Anyone could have seen the person do it."

"Except if it was done at night," Chief Martin said. "Most of the residents don't stay out late. Someone probably decided to drop off a syringe when the house was pretty dark. Lots of shadows to hide in."

"Do you think this person is toying with Megan?" Angie asked. "Trying to frighten her?"

"I'd have to guess *yes*," the chief said.

"What's the point of trying to scare her?" Jenna asked. "By now, she's told law enforcement everything she knows about Perry."

"To throw her off, to make her frightened, to

keep her mind busy so she doesn't piece things together to point to a killer," Chief Martin said.

"Do you think Megan knows something?" Jenna asked.

"Not necessarily, but I think it deserves paying attention to." Chief Martin stepped to the side for a few minutes to speak with an officer.

Jenna moved closer to her sister. "Do *you* think Megan knows something?"

"I'm not sure what to think," Angie admitted. "Megan could have planted the syringe in her mailbox to make her appear innocent, to make it seem that someone has it in for her."

The chief returned to the young women. "Someone is coming by soon to pick up the syringe for testing. I'm going to allow myself some optimism and hope there are some fingerprints on the syringe."

"Longshot," Angie said. "But they may as well try. Clues aren't exactly numerous, are they?"

"I'm not all that hopeful," Jenna said. "Whoever did this didn't zoom over here half-baked. It would be very lax behavior to leave behind a print on the syringe." She glanced to the front door. "You think whoever left the syringe lives in this house?"

"It would make sense," the chief said. "He or she

wouldn't have had far to go to get to the mailbox and leave a surprise for Megan. However, I'm not dismissing the fact that this could have been done by someone living outside the house."

"Maybe it was the person who was with Andy Hobbs the night of Perry's murder?" Angie asked. "Did that person place the item in Megan's mailbox? I agree that it could be a warning. Maybe Perry's killer wants to murder Megan, too, and is trying to freak her out before he strikes."

"Maybe playing a little game of cat and mouse," the chief said.

"Where is Megan now?" Jenna asked.

"She's inside with an officer," the chief said.

"Angie brought up a good point. What if Megan put the syringe in her own mailbox," Jenna asked. "What if Megan is actually Perry's killer and she is trying to throw suspicion off of herself."

"She could have made up the story about kissing Perry the night he died," Angie said. "She might have made it up to make her seem vulnerable, to get my sympathy. To keep me from thinking that Megan is the killer."

"What about Andy Hobbs?" Jenna asked. "He could have accessed Megan's mail. He seems to have his nose in a bunch of different places."

"There's something that bothers me," Angie revealed. "Megan made a move on Perry shortly before he died. She kissed him when they were standing in front of the big windows of Perry's room. It was dark, but the room was lit. If anyone was watching, that person certainly could have thought Perry and Megan were involved in a relationship."

"If jealousy was the motive," Jenna said, "seeing the kiss might have fueled the killer's rage."

"Have you talked to Andy Hobbs about who he was speaking with at the back door of the house?" Angie asked.

"Andy was away for a couple of days," the chief said. "He's going to have a chat with me in about ten minutes. Will you talk to Megan when she's done with the officer? See what you can find out? I asked her to come out here when she's done inside."

Angie and Jenna agreed just as Andy Hobbs stepped out onto the porch carrying a dark brown briefcase.

"Morning." Hobbs nodded to the sisters and his gaze sent a cold chill racing over Angie's skin. He turned to Chief Martin and asked, "Are you ready? I don't have a lot of time right now. I need to get to school."

Chief Martin and Hobbs went inside to find a private place to have their discussion.

"I don't like that guy," Jenna sniffed. "He's arrogant and self-important."

"He worries me," Angie said. "He seems like trouble."

As Angie and Jenna shared their concerns about Andy Hobbs, Megan came onto the porch to find the sisters. With the rims of her eyes red and her face pale, she looked shaky and unsettled.

"Chief Martin asked me to talk to you." Megan's voice was soft and weak.

"Why don't we go sit on the side porch," Angie suggested.

The sun's rays warmed the wide, white veranda which overlooked the rocky cliffs and the shimmering blue ocean and the beauty of the view almost pushed away the worry and alarm created by the morning's event. Almost.

Megan took in a long breath and said in a shaking voice, "Now someone is after me. Now someone wants me dead. Why? What's going on? Is the killer going to murder every person who lives in this house or does he have some grudge against only me and Perry? What did either of us do wrong?"

There were no answers to Megan's questions so

Angie focused on the syringe. "When did you find the syringe?"

"This morning. I was up early to do some studying. I made breakfast, wrote a couple of bills. I went out to my mailbox to put the envelopes inside for mailing and I saw I'd left two pieces of mail in the box from last night. The syringe was wrapped in one of the flyers."

"You checked your mailbox last night?" Angie asked.

"I got home late. It was dark. I grabbed my mail and went inside to my room. I guess I missed a couple of things," Megan said.

"What were the things you left behind?"

"Only two flyers. They must have been pushed to the back and I didn't see them."

"Or you didn't leave any mail behind and the person who left the syringe put the flyers in to help hide it," Angie said. "I'm guessing the person came with the syringe during the night so it would be easier to access the box without being seen."

"I didn't think of that," Megan said as she rubbed at her temple.

"Has anyone made any comments to you that you might consider threatening in light of receiving the syringe?" Jenna asked.

Megan blinked, her facial expression blank as she considered the question. "I don't think so. No, I can't think of anything. What should I do? Should I hire some guy to walk around with me for protection?"

"Chief Martin will take care of that if he thinks it's necessary," Angie said in a comforting tone. "Sometimes they have an officer nearby as you go about your day just as a precaution."

Megan sank down onto one of the chaise lounges and held her head in her hands. "Why is this happening?" She sat up. "I'm not going to classes today. I'm staying here for the day. I need to be somewhere I feel safe. Do you think it's okay to take the day off? I can't face walking around campus or sitting in classes."

"I think it's perfectly fine," Jenna told the frightened young woman.

Angie agreed with her sister, but a nagging sense of unease pricked at her and filled her heart with dread.

24

Angie, Jenna, and Chief Martin sat together in Maribeth's office in the boarding house.

"I have two things to report," the chief said while running his hand through his hair. "First, Andy Hobbs tells me he was *not* in the yard on the night Perry was killed. He did not enter the house through the back door."

Angie's mouth dropped open. "What?"

"Andy told me he always goes in through the front door. His room is upstairs and the staircase leads off the foyer so why would he enter through the rear?"

"He's lying," Angie huffed.

"I asked him who he was with and he told me he was alone," the chief said.

"This is ridiculous. Mary Bishop saw him." Angie's blue eyes flashed.

"Andy said he doesn't care who told me he was in the backyard," the chief told them. "Andy said the person or persons who claim to have seen him are mistaken. It wasn't him out there."

"He said this with a straight face?" Jenna's eyes had narrowed. "He didn't look guilty or twitchy or fidgety? Did he meet your eyes when he talked?"

"He didn't look nervous, but he did look annoyed with my questions, and yes, he made eye contact."

"Was he sweating? Did he do anything that might have indicated he was lying?" Angie asked.

"No sweating. No looking away. The man does come off as superior and he shows contempt for my questioning, but those things aren't enough to assume he's lying."

"He's lying." Angie's heart pounded with frustration and anger. "I can feel it."

"There are no security cameras outside so all we have is one person's word against another." The chief shrugged a shoulder and looked at Angie. "That doesn't mean we won't keep an eye on Andy Hobbs, especially since you ... you know, sense he isn't telling the truth."

"You didn't mention Mary Bishop was the one who saw Hobbs at the door that night, did you?" Angie asked.

"I did not, but I'm sure Hobbs can figure it out since Mary's window is the only one with a good view of the back steps," the chief said.

A look of worry came over Angie's face. "We should warn her."

"I'll speak with her before I leave," Chief Martin said.

"You said there were two things you wanted to tell us," Jenna said.

"Investigators have gone through security tapes of the med school library. A couple of the cameras weren't working and one tape from the front door of the place is missing."

Angie groaned.

"The tapes that are available do not show Charles Conte in the library after 10pm."

"So Charles was either not in the library after ten or he was there, but in one of the sections where the security cameras weren't working," Jenna said. "That's not very definitive."

"No, it isn't," the chief agreed. "Road blocks at

every turn. Officers are talking to students and other people who use the med school library on a regular basis asking if they remember Charles in the library after 10pm on the night of Perry's murder."

"Maybe someone will have seen him in there during the window of time Perry was killed," Angie said. "Then we'll know for certain that Charles can be taken off the suspect list."

"What about Perry's former girlfriend, Maura Norris?" Jenna asked. "We haven't talked to her in a week. Have the investigators looked into where she was that night? Have they been able to cross her off the list of suspects?"

"Maura reported she was alone in her apartment in Boston the night Perry died," Chief Martin said. "No one can confirm or deny her whereabouts."

A frown formed on Jenna's lips. "Where do we go from here?"

"We'll keep sniffing out leads and following up on them," the chief said.

∼

ON THE WAY back to the Victorian, Angie asked Jenna, "Want to take a little detour down to the resort?"

"You want to drop in on Josh?"

"I want to sit on the Point for a few minutes. Things are a jumble in my head and I'm not picking up on things the way I usually can. I need Nana's help."

Jenna headed the car down to the Sweet Cove Resort, parked in the lot, and she and her sister walked over to Robin's Point, a spit of grassy land that jutted out into the Atlantic Ocean over the colorful cliffs. When Josh and his brother purchased the resort, they made a park on the Point so that people could enjoy the view and access the path down to the small beach.

The Roselands' nana had once owned a cottage on the point where the sisters had stayed for weeks each summer when they were children. The cottage was gone now, but Josh arranged to return a parcel of land to each of the four sisters to do with whatever they wished. So far, they were simply content to have the land in the family again with no plans to build on any of it.

In the mid-morning sun, Angie and Jenna settled on the soft, green grass at the edge of the cliff and watched the gulls soar overhead and the waves crash on the beach below.

"I always feel peaceful when I'm here." Angie

pulled her hair up into a loose bun and rested back on the grass. "I feel close to Nana here. I can feel her heart pulsing in my veins."

"I feel the same way," Jenna said, pulling her legs up under her. "A lot has changed since we were kids here. We've all developed powers like Nana. We're all running businesses. You and I are married. Ellie and Courtney will probably marry their boyfriends. We have the Victorian. We have Mr. Finch in our lives."

Without opening her eyes, Angie smiled and said, "And we have two smart, special cats in our lives, too."

"That's right." Jenna listened to the waves pounding the sand. "I'd say things are pretty good."

"I'd say you're right." Angie's breathing was slow and relaxed. "There's one thing that hasn't changed."

"What's that?" Jenna asked.

"The four of us are still all together," Angie said.

"That better not ever change."

Angie said, "I wish Mel and Cora weren't away on vacation. I'd like to talk to them about this case. See if they might be able to give us some tips."

A middle-aged couple, Mel and Cora Abel met when they were both staying as guests at the bed and breakfast in the Victorian, fell in love, and decided to buy a house together in the pretty seaside town. Cora had strong paranormal powers and had helped the sisters better understand what they could do.

"They'll be back in a week, but that might not be soon enough," Jenna said. "Aren't you getting your hair cut this afternoon? Why don't you talk to Gloria?"

Angie sat up. "You know Gloria doesn't like to talk about *skills*."

Gloria owned a hair salon in town and also had paranormal powers, but unlike Cora, Gloria was closed-lipped about her abilities. She once helped the sisters when someone tried to kill them by setting the carriage house on fire, but that was the only time she'd admitted to having powers. When Angie brought it up one day, Gloria quickly shut down the discussion.

"Well, beat around the bush with her," Jenna said. "Maybe if you ask things in an indirect way, Gloria will answer your questions."

Angie narrowed her eyes at her sister. "Or she'll toss me out of the salon with only one side of my hair cut."

Jenna chuckled. "It's worth a try. Ellie can even your hair out if necessary."

"I don't know," Angie said. "I don't want to make her angry."

"Feel her out. Go slowly. She might soften if you explain what a hard time we're having trying to help Chief Martin with the case."

"How about you go in my place?" Angie asked.

"Um, no thanks." Jenna smiled. "You'll be much better at it than I would be."

"I'm not falling for false flattery. Why don't you come with me? We can both chat up Gloria while she cuts my hair."

"Nope. This is best done one on one," Jenna said. "So I'll wish you luck."

Angie sighed and asked, "Shall we head back to work? Louisa will send out a search party if I don't get back to the bake shop soon."

"Maybe we should just take the day off and sit here in the sun," Jenna suggested as she stood up.

"I don't think that idea will fly," Angie said.

Jenna held out her hand to help her sister off the grass and when they were both standing, Angie stared at their hands with wide eyes.

"Did you feel that?" Angie asked.

"Yeah, what was it?" Jenna removed her hand from her sister's and looked at her skin. "It felt like a huge electrical surge between us."

"The heat was intense. It felt like fire," Angie said. "That was really weird."

"That's never happened before." Jenna was still looking at the skin on her hand to see if there might be slight burn marks.

"What does it mean?" Angie asked. "Why did it happen?"

Jenna looked at her twin sister and reached out for her hands. "Let's see if it happens again."

Angie slowly lifted her arms and slipped her hands into Jenna's.

"Nothing," Jenna said with disappointment.

"Wait," Angie said. "I feel something."

"Oh. It's starting again."

Heat began to build coming from the inside of their hands with a slight vibrating sensation added to the unusual feeling.

A smile spread over Jenna's face. "It's powerful. But what is it?"

"It makes me feel ... strong." Angie returned her sister's smile. "Is it from Nana?"

"Whatever it is, I like it. It makes me feel closer to you than ever." Jenna dropped Angie's hands and wrapped her arms around her sister in a warm, sweet, loving embrace.

25
___

Angie sat in the salon chair in front of the big mirror on the wall of Gloria's spacious, modern recently expanded hair salon. The walls were done in creamy, light grey, the newly-refinished wood floors sparkled under the fancy light fixtures, and leather chairs and sofas clustered together near a gas fireplace in the waiting area.

"The place looks beautiful," Angie said.

"It better. It cost a bundle." Gloria ran a comb through Angie's shoulder-length hair. "Just a trim and a shaping today?"

"Yes, please."

Angie and the hairstylist caught up on what had been going on since the last time Angie had been in.

Gloria had spent the past six weeks stressed out over the renovations by trying to keep one side open while the other side was being worked on.

"It was a mess. The clients were good about it, but it really bothered me. You're lucky you weren't scheduled for a haircut during those weeks. The storage areas had been ripped out, everything was spread all over the place and we couldn't find our supplies. It was a real headache," Gloria said with a sigh. "I'd never go through it again."

"But it's gorgeous now," Angie told her. "You must think it was worth it?"

"I guess you have to take the bitter with the sweet," Gloria said with shrug.

Angie's eyes widened. "I've heard that saying about four times in the last week."

Gloria smiled and snipped the ends of a few strands of hair. "Really? It's not that common. Everyone must be thinking alike right now."

"You've heard about the death at Maribeth's boarding house?" Angie brought up the subject she hoped to speak with Gloria about.

"Awful, isn't it? I haven't seen Maribeth since it happened. How is she doing?"

"She's holding up despite feeling responsible. She's berating herself for not keeping one of her boarders safe. She's dealing with a lot of guilt over it."

"It's not Maribeth's fault." Gloria held two strands of hair in the air to judge if they were the same length. "Maribeth runs a tight ship over there. She's very careful about safety, security, and making a pleasant environment for everyone in the house."

"I keep telling her that," Angie said. "But until the crime is solved, no one living there is going to feel safe."

"Are you helping Chief Martin?" Gloria asked, keeping her voice down.

"We are, but we're all coming up empty." Angie made eye contact with the woman in the mirror hoping Gloria would realize that she could really use some help.

Gloria asked a few questions and Angie explained some of the details of the case, the suspects, the linguist's determination about the suicide letter's use of language, a resident of the house seeing two people at the back door on the night Perry was killed, and one of those people's denial of being in the rear yard that evening. She also told about the syringe in Megan's mailbox.

"It's like a ball of yarn with all the threads mixed up together," Angie said.

"Hmm." Gloria seemed to be deep in thought, and then she asked, "Have you been in the backyard of the boarding house?"

"Only briefly."

"Can you describe it to me?"

Angie did so. "And there's a path that splits with one side going down to the beach and the other side going around to the front of the house."

"Have you been on the paths?" Gloria asked.

The thought that she hadn't been thorough enough raced around in Angie's head, and she sheepishly admitted, "No, I haven't been on the paths."

"It couldn't hurt I suppose." Gloria seemed distracted. "Although the police must have walked around back there." The woman gave herself a little shake and picked up a different pair of scissors. "Anyway, something will come up that will help resolve the case."

Angie decided to bring something else up. "When I was in the deceased's bedroom, I smelled an odor. It was almost a medicinal smell. Sometimes, it makes me feel ill."

Gloria lowered the comb and leaned closer to Angie's ear. "You might be picking up on something the killer left behind."

"I wondered about that. Would I be able to smell the same thing if I was close to the person responsible for Perry's death?"

"You might, but I believe it would be only the tiniest wisp of the odor. It would be very easy to miss it. In the heat of the moment of taking someone's life, the killer left a trace of his energy behind and you're picking up on it with your sense of smell. Keep on your toes. If the killer is in a frenzy to kill again, he or she will most likely emit the same odor. Pay attention to scents on the air, however slight," Gloria said.

Angie nodded and thanked Gloria for her advice.

AFTER LEAVING THE SALON, Angie decided to take a detour over to the boarding house to look around the backyard and follow the paths behind the property. She phoned Maribeth to tell her she would be in the garden, but the woman didn't answer so she left a message.

The day was unusually warm for the time of year and perspiration ran down Angie's back as she walked through town to the road where the boarding house was located. The street was narrow with mature trees on both sides and large expensive homes, many set back behind high hedges, lined the lane. Approaching the boarding house, Angie was grateful for the cool shade as she turned onto the pathway that wound between the shrubbery and around to the back of the home.

Before branching off down the hill to the ocean, the dirt path led to the left to a white arbor set in between the tall, dark green hedges that ran around the periphery of the boarding house's property.

Angie stood at the gate glancing around the yard. No one was outside so she turned and took the path down the hill through the trees until the trail turned rocky when it cut between and over the cliffs. Moving carefully so as not to trip or slip, Angie finally reached the tiny, soft sand beach where she stood looking out over the water.

Several minutes passed before Angie turned to head back up to the house and her heart dropped when she realized how steep the climb would be. Taking a deep breath, she started up the hill, but stopped short.

She could see part of the long, white veranda-like porch that jutted off the side of the boarding house and two people were standing there, talking.

One was Megan. Angie squinted and shaded her eyes from the sun's glare.

The other person looked like Charles Conte.

Angie frowned thinking Charles must be pestering Megan once again, but suddenly the thought disappeared with the racing of her heart.

She took off running up the path.

Reaching the arbor and breathing hard, Angie bent over at the waist to catch her breath from her dash up the long, pebbly hill and when she began to straighten up, something under the brush caught her eye.

Pushing under the branches, Angie leaned down to see what it was.

She picked it up.

A book about the impact of anesthesia on cardiac surgery.

Angie's vision dimmed. It was the book Charles Conte borrowed from Perry on the night the young man was murdered.

Under a bush? Oh, no.

Taking a half-second to consider her options, Angie ran along the path to the front of the house and before following the brick walkway from the front door to the side of the house where the steps led up onto the wide veranda, she pulled out her phone and sent Chief Martin a text.

Come to the boarding house. Hurry.

Then she climbed the stairs to the porch, and when she reached the deck, a wisp of the medicinal odor she'd smelled in Perry's room wafted under her nose. *Charles.*

Charles's back was to Angie as he faced Megan. Angie couldn't hear what he was saying to her, but from the terrified look on Megan's face, she grasped the meaning.

Forcing a smile, Angie loudly greeted the two people.

Charles spun around and gaped at the unexpected visitor. "What are you doing here?"

Spotting the syringe in the man's hand, Angie moved slowly over the porch deck trying to get closer to Megan. "I could ask you the same question."

"Stop moving," Charles demanded.

Angie obeyed, but she made eye contact with the shaking woman several yards away from her.

"What are you doing, Charles?" Angie asked trying to buy time until the chief arrived. "Aren't you in enough trouble? Don't add to it."

"You don't know." Charles's eyes were wild and wide and spittle showed at the corners of his mouth.

"I do know. Why don't you put the syringe down and move away from it?" Angie used a calm voice to try and reason with the man.

"Why don't you shut up?"

Angie shuffled a few more feet towards Megan.

"I told you not to move," Charles roared.

Out of the corner of her eye, Angie saw Megan, looking dazed, slip slowly down to the porch floor and lean back against the railing.

The sun beat down on them like a white-hot laser beam.

Angie took a look at Megan sprawled like a drunk and then asked Charles, "What did you do to her?"

Charles sneered and held up the hand holding the syringe. "I didn't do anything to her. Yet."

Angie moved to stand in front of Megan.

"I bet I have enough in here to kill both of you." Charles's voice was eerily soft.

Angie could see the man's cheeks were flushed and his chest was rapidly rising up and down. She knew he was on the verge of lunging at them. Her heart pounded like a sledgehammer.

Trying to remain calm, she forced the words

from her tight throat. "Stay where you are. Put the syringe down." *How are we going to get out of this?*

Sweat dripped from Charles's forehead.

Angie wanted to kneel and check on Megan, but she didn't dare, thinking her movement would set Charles in motion. "Megan?" She turned her head slightly to see if the young woman was conscious.

Megan looked up at Angie with fear-darkened eyes.

"Get ready to fight," Angie whispered ... and she balled her fists and hunched down slightly waiting for Charles to pounce.

The man lunged holding the syringe like a weapon and just before he plowed into Angie, she side-stepped him and swung her arm attempting to knock the thing from his hand, but Charles dove at Megan to inject her.

"Roll!" Angie yelled.

As Megan rolled onto her side away from her attacker, Angie kicked at Charles's arm dislodging the syringe, and then she lost her balance and fell backwards with a crashing thud that sent stars flashing in her eyes.

"Police! Hold it right there! Don't move!" Chief Martin was on the porch with his gun drawn and when Angie looked up at him from her position on her back, she burst into tears of relief.

Still holding the gun on Charles who froze on the deck in front of the law enforcement officer, Chief Martin knelt next to Angie.

"You okay?" his voice quavered as he looked her over for injuries.

"I'm perfect," Angie blubbered as she sat up, a strand of hair stuck on her wet cheek.

The worry disappeared from the chief's face and he smiled while tugging a handkerchief from his back pocket. He handed it to Angie before standing to go check on Megan and take Charles into custody.

"Most people don't begin to sob when they see me," the chief kidded.

"Most people aren't me." Angie wiped at her eyes with his handkerchief.

"Thank the heavens for that." Chief Martin squeezed Angie's shoulder. "Because my poor old heart couldn't take it."

26

"I feel badly for thinking Megan may have killed Perry," Angie said as she started the fire pit in the garden of the Victorian. The family had spent the day at the beach, bodysurfing, swimming, floating on inner tubes, and sunning themselves on the white sand beach.

"Don't feel badly. We all thought she might have done it." Jenna had just finished lighting the torches around the yard.

"No one is innocent until proven so," Courtney reminded everyone.

"Not exactly how our justice system works, but I know what you mean," Ellie said with a smile.

Courtney explained, "When someone is in a courtroom, it's the other way around, but when we're investigating a crime, we have to consider everyone a suspect until we can rule them out."

"It's true, Miss Courtney." Finch and Betty were setting the table under the pergola and little white lights twinkled over the top and down the sides of the poles. "We can't overlook anyone when there is a crime to solve."

Euclid and Circe sat together in one of the Adirondack chairs listening to the conversation.

Rufus came out of the house carrying a cooler full of drinks and set it down near the side table on the patio before picking up a wine glass. "What can I get everyone to drink?"

Chief Martin and his wife, Lucille, gave Rufus their orders and were soon sipping from their glasses.

"Megan is feeling very guilty," Chief Martin told the group. "She thinks if she'd told Perry how Charles was behaving towards her, he might have been more careful around him. I don't think it would have mattered one way or the other. Charles Conte was unstable, but no one really knew how truly disturbed he was."

Tom came out of the back door carrying a platter of raw burgers, chicken kabobs, and veggie burgers. "Can you go over what happened the night Perry was killed? I've heard bits and pieces, but I haven't been told the whole story."

"I'd like to hear it as well," Jack Ford followed behind Tom carrying a tray with a bowl of salad, a bowl of potato salad, condiments, a plate of cut-up fruit, and a lemon-berry cake which he set on the long patio table.

Chief Martin began the sorry tale while Josh fired up the grill. "Andy Hobbs denies having any role in Perry's death. He still says he was not in the backyard of the boarding house the night Perry died. He claims he didn't see or speak with Charles."

"But Charles reports Andy did talk with him," Ellie said. "And in fact, fed his fury and indignation over seeing Megan and Perry in the window kissing that night."

Angie picked up the story. "Charles went to Perry's room to borrow a book. He ran into Megan when he left the boarding house and he tried to kiss her. She reminded him that they would never date as Charles wasn't her type. She told him Perry was her type which began a fire of fury building within Charles. Megan went inside and ran into Perry who was about to go to bed. Megan went into Perry's room to talk, but she ended up revealing her feelings for Perry and even kissed him after confessing how she felt about him. Charles was lurking in the backyard and saw the kiss through Perry's windows. He paced around the yard and when he was leaving through the gate under the arbor, he threw the book he'd borrowed under a bush."

Jenna said, "Charles told law enforcement that Andy Hobbs arrived at the arbor as he was about to leave. Andy saw how upset he was and Charles told him what had happened. Andy fed into Charles's rage and even said that Perry was an awful person who didn't deserve to live. Charles agreed and asked Andy to let him into the house. Andy told him he wasn't allowed to let anyone in at that time of night, but Charles should watch him as he went in. Charles saw Andy get the hidden key to the door."

"Charles decided to finish Perry off," Courtney said. "He knew Perry kept the medication and syringes in his dresser in the sitting room so he took the hidden key, entered the house, and went to Perry's room. Perry never locked his door so getting inside was no problem for Charles. Charles took the full syringe to Perry's bedroom and injected him with the overdose. He wanted to do the same to Megan, but the door to her room was locked."

Chief Martin said, "Perry planned to kill Megan

later and he would have if Angie hadn't arrived when she did."

"What about the suicide note?" Rufus asked.

"So Charles wrote the note on Perry's laptop?" Josh asked.

"Charles claims he did not write it," Chief Martin said. "Although Andy denies having any part in the death, we believe he snuck into Perry's room after Charles left the house and wrote the suicide note to keep investigators from thinking Perry had been murdered."

"I remember when we were at the boarding house having dinner with the residents," Courtney said. "Andy was going on about how Mary Bishop shouldn't be included with the rest of them as workers in the medical field. He said Mary didn't understand medical terms and started to argue about it. Roger Winthrop told him he was being too picky and to let it go. Andy said something like using correct language was important."

"We should have picked up on that," Angie said. "Using correct grammar and accurate vocabulary was important to Andy just like the linguist we met told us the author of the note would be. She said the writer of the note was very specific in his use of language."

"We missed that," Jenna said. "We blew it."

"In retrospect," Finch said, "it is easy to pick up on it. Not so in real life. It got missed in all the conversation that night."

"We need to be sharper in the future," Angie said.

"Charles will be charged with Perry's murder," Ellie said. "But will Andy be charged with anything since he inflamed Charles and probably wrote the suicide note?"

Chief Martin let out a sigh. "Not unless we find any evidence he had a role. As of right now, Andy gets off free and clear. It isn't a crime to incite anyone."

"That seems so wrong." Jenna's eyes darkened in anger.

"There's nothing that can be done," the chief said resignedly.

"Perry's killer has been caught and justice will be served," Finch said. "Unfortunately, we have to accept that Andy may never be punished for his role. Sometimes, we have to take the good with the bad."

"You're right, Mr. Finch," Courtney said. "But I don't like it."

"Let's talk about something other than bad guys

and murder," Tom suggested as he helped Josh take the food off the grill.

Josh piped up, "Angie has some good news to tell."

All eyes turned to the young woman.

Angie smiled. "I've decided to accept the museum's offer to have the second bake shop there."

Euclid and Circe trilled as a cheer went up from the group and each friend and family member took a turn giving Angie a congratulatory hug.

"I'm so glad, sis," Courtney squeezed her sister. "I'm happy you decided to do it."

Angie said, "I've promoted Louisa to manager of the stores. She's a great worker and friend and I want her to have a bigger role in running the shops with me."

"Louisa really is like your right-hand man," Jenna said. "Or should I say right-hand woman."

Everyone chuckled and then sat down to dinner under the pretty white lights and with the torches casting a lovely golden glow around the yard.

For dessert, the group made s'mores and stood with their long metal kabob skewers toasting marshmallows over the fire pit. Betty and Lucille carried some dishes into the kitchen to put in the dishwasher.

"The weirdest thing happened when Angie and I were at Robin's Point the other day." Jenna explained how they'd held hands and felt a burning sensation building under their skin.

"Really?" Ellie looked at her sisters with apprehension.

"Let's try." Courtney set down her skewer and took Angie's hands in her hers. After waiting a few moments, she said, "Nothing's happening. How long did it take to work?"

"Only a second or two," Jenna said.

Rufus shook his head as he went into the house to get another bottle of wine. "You all act like you believe in magic or something."

Courtney winked at her sisters. "Or something."

"My hands aren't getting hot this time," Angie said with a disappointed expression.

"Let me try." Jenna moved close to Angie and took her hands, and in three seconds their faces lit up. "I feel it," Jenna said.

"Let me see." Courtney quickly stepped in front of Jenna and took Angie's hands. "Your hands are hot!"

Tom chuckled. "The latest Roseland-sister trick."

"Let me hold her hands," Ellie said taking a turn. "It doesn't feel like much. It's not that warm."

"It's fading because Jenna let go of me," Angie explained.

"Why doesn't it work when Ellie or I hold you?" Courtney pouted. "Why is it working only for you and Jenna?"

"I have no idea," Angie said.

"It's cool though, isn't it?" Jenna asked with a grin.

"I think you mean it's hot." Jack smiled.

Euclid and Circe padded over and stared at the twin sisters, then let out loud meows.

Josh came over to Angie and put his arm around her shoulders. "I think the cats are trying to figure it out."

"Well, when someone has the answer, let the rest of us know." Courtney picked up her skewer, pushed two marshmallows onto the stick, and stepped over to the fire pit while some of the others did the same.

Tom and Jenna came over to stand with Angie and Josh and the foursome chatted about the day at the beach and about maybe going on a bike ride together in the morning.

While they talked, Josh moved closer to his wife and absentmindedly placed his left hand gently on Angie's stomach. She put her hand over Josh's and then she stared across the yard for a moment before making eye contact with Mr. Finch who sat in an Adirondack chair with the two cats next to him.

Finch's eyes twinkled and he smiled at Angie.

A thought popped into the young woman's head and she looked down at her and Josh's hands still resting on her stomach. Angie quickly looked over to Mr. Finch and when their eyes met, she knew. A wide smile spread over her lips, and then she paused suddenly and stared with wide eyes at Jenna's stomach.

Flicking her gaze back to Finch and the cats, Angie's face wore a questioning expression. Finch nodded at her and the two of them broke out in beaming smiles.

Angie turned to Josh, put her hands on the sides of his face, and gave him a long, loving kiss.

Josh grinned. "Well, what did I do to deserve that?"

Angie took a step closer to her twin and surprised her sister when she put her hand onto Jenna's stomach and then wrapped her in a bear hug.

For a few moments, Angie and Finch and the two fine felines were the only ones who knew what was going on.

Turning back to Josh, Angie whispered in his ear. "I know why Jenna and I feel the fire in us."

Josh looked confused for a second, and then realization dawned on him. When he looked down at her stomach, he reached for Angie's hands, and as the words he wanted to say got stuck in his throat, a tear of joy tumbled down his cheek.

And on that warm, lovely night with the stars shining overhead, one orange cat and one black one let out howls of happiness into the sweet summer air.

THANK YOU FOR READING! RECIPES BELOW!

Books by J.A. WHITING can be found here:
www.amazon.com/author/jawhiting

To hear about new books and book sales, please sign up for my mailing list at:
www.jawhitingbooks.com

Your email will never be sold, shared, or spammed.

If you enjoyed the book, please consider leaving a review. A few words are all that's needed. It would be very much appreciated.

BOOKS/SERIES BY J. A. WHITING

CLAIRE ROLLINS COZY MYSTERY SERIES

PAXTON PARK COZY MYSTERIES

LIN COFFIN COZY MYSTERY SERIES

SWEET COVE COZY MYSTERY SERIES

OLIVIA MILLER MYSTERY-THRILLER SERIES
(not cozy)

ABOUT THE AUTHOR

J.A. Whiting lives with her family in New England.
Whiting loves reading and writing mystery stories.

Visit me at:

www.jawhitingbooks.com
www.bookbub.com/authors/j-a-whiting
www.amazon.com/author/jawhiting
www.facebook.com/jawhitingauthor

SOME RECIPES FROM THE SWEET COVE SERIES

SUMMER LEMON BERRY CAKE

INGREDIENTS FOR CAKE

- 1⅓ cups all-purpose flour
- ½ cup granulated sugar
- 2 teaspoons baking powder
- ¼ teaspoon salt
- 1 large egg, room temperature
- ⅔ cup buttermilk
- ⅓ cup butter, melted
- 1 teaspoon grated lemon zest
- 1¼ tablespoon lemon juice
- 1½ teaspoon vanilla extract
- 1 cup sliced strawberries

INGREDIENTS FOR TOPPING

- 1 cup fresh blackberries

1 cup sliced strawberries

1 tablespoon lemon juice

¾ teaspoon sugar

2 cups whipped cream

DIRECTIONS FOR CAKE

Preheat the oven to 350 degrees F.

Grease and flour a 9 inch round baking pan.

In a large bowl, mix flour, sugar, baking powder, and salt.

In a bowl, whisk egg, buttermilk, melted butter, lemon zest, lemon juice, and vanilla, then add to the dry ingredients.

Stir mixture until just moistened.

Fold in 1 cup of strawberries.

Pour into the prepared pan.

Bake for 20-25 minutes (or until toothpick comes out clean).

Cool 15 minutes.

Remove from pan.

DIRECTIONS FOR TOPPING

Toss berries with the lemon juice and sugar.

Spread whipped cream over the top.

Top with the berries!

EASY EVERYTHING-BROWNIES

INGREDIENTS

1 box fudge brownie mix

2 eggs

1 stick butter, and

3 tablespoons water

¾ cup dark chocolate chips

¼ cup cookie and cream cookies, broken into pieces

¼ cup mini pretzels, broken into pieces

7-9 peanut butter cups, chopped

DIRECTIONS

Preheat the oven to 350 degrees F.

Spray an 8 X 8 inch baking dish with nonstick baking spray.

In a large bowl, mix together brownie mix, eggs, 1 stick softened butter, and water. Pour the batter into the prepared pan.

Bake for 50 minutes or until a toothpick inserted into the center comes out clean. Cool completely.

Using a microwave safe bowl, microwave the chocolate chips and the 6 tablespoons butter until melted. Stir until the mixture is smooth and spread over the brownies.

Top with the cookies, pretzels, and peanut butter cups.

Put into the refrigerator until the topping sets.

Slice into squares.

SUGAR COOKIES

INGREDIENTS

2½ cups all-purpose flour

1½ teaspoons baking powder

½ teaspoon salt

1 cup (2 sticks) unsalted butter, room temperature

2 cups granulated sugar

2 large eggs

1½ teaspoons vanilla

DIRECTIONS

Preheat the oven to 350 degrees F.

In a medium bowl, mix flour, baking powder, and salt.

Using an electric mixer, beat butter and sugar

on medium-high speed until fluffy, about 3 minutes.

One at time, beat in the eggs, and then add the vanilla.

Reduce speed to low, gradually add in flour moisture, mixing until just combined.

Drop hearty tablespoons of dough onto the baking sheet, space them 2 inches apart.

Bake until cookies are golden, about 13-15 minutes, rotate the baking sheet hallway through the baking.

Cool for 5 minutes on baking sheet, then move to wire rack to cool completely.

Store in container for up to 5 days.

RASPBERRY COOLER CAKE

INGREDIENTS

26 graham crackers, crushed

½ cup butter

¼ cup packed brown sugar

1 6-ounce package of raspberry flavored Jello ® mix

1 cup boiling water

15 ounces frozen raspberries

22 large marshmallows

⅓ cup milk

1 cup heavy whipping cream, whipped

DIRECTIONS

Preheat the oven to 350 degrees F.

Mix graham crackers, butter, and brown sugar

until combined. Set aside ¼ cup of the mixture for a topping. Press the remainder of the mixture into a 9 X 13 inch pan.

Bake for 10 minutes; let cool.

Dissolve the raspberry gelatin in the boiling water and add in the frozen raspberries, stir until melted. Chill until partially set. Spread on the graham cracker base.

Melt the marshmallows together with the milk. When cooled, fold in the whipped cream and then spread over the top of the raspberry mixture.

Sprinkle with the graham cracker topping.

Chill for about 3-4 hours before serving.

Enjoy!

Made in the USA
Middletown, DE
04 July 2023